audition

audition

STASIA WARD KEHOE

VIKING
An Imprint of Penguin Group (USA) Inc.

VIKING
Published by Penguin Group
Penguin Group (USA) Inc., 345 Hudson Street, New York, New York 10014, U.S.A.
Penguin Group (Canada), 90 Eglinton Avenue East, Suite 700, Toronto, Ontario, Canada M4P 2Y3 (a division of Pearson Penguin Canada Inc.)
Penguin Books Ltd, 80 Strand, London WC2R 0RL, England
Penguin Ireland, 25 St Stephen's Green, Dublin 2, Ireland (a division of Penguin Books Ltd)
Penguin Group (Australia), 250 Camberwell Road, Camberwell, Victoria 3124, Australia (a division of Pearson Australia Group Pty Ltd)
Penguin Books India Pvt Ltd, 11 Community Centre, Panchsheel Park, New Delhi – 110 017, India
Penguin Group (NZ), 67 Apollo Drive, Rosedale, Auckland 0632, New Zealand (a division of Pearson New Zealand Ltd.)
Penguin Books (South Africa) (Pty) Ltd, 24 Sturdee Avenue, Rosebank, Johannesburg 2196, South Africa

Penguin Books Ltd, Registered Offices: 80 Strand, London WC2R 0RL, England

First published in 2011 by Viking, a member of Penguin Group (USA) Inc.

10 9 8 7 6 5 4 3 2 1

LIBRARY OF CONGRESS CATALOGING-IN-PUBLICATION DATA
Ward, S. (Stasia), date-
Audition : a verse novel / by Stasia Ward Kehoe.
p. cm.
Summary: When sixteen-year-old Sara, from a small Vermont town, wins a scholarship to study ballet in New Jersey, her ambivalence about her future increases even as her dancing improves.
ISBN 978-0-670-01319-7 (hardcover : alk. paper) [1. Novels in verse. 2. Ballet dancing—Fiction. 3. Interpersonal relations—Fiction.] I. Title.
PZ7.5.W24Au 2011
[Fic]—dc22
2010044307

Printed in U.S.A. — Set in Joulliard — Book design by Kate Renner

In loving memory of
Kevin James Kehoe, Sr.,
and Charlotte Elizabeth Eck

ACKNOWLEDGMENTS

The dance, drama, and school teachers who opened my mind to the stories I could tell on stage and on paper . . .

SCBWI Western Washington, a generous, hard-working group of writers, through which I connected with awesome beta-readers Molly and Dawn . . .

My agent, Catherine Drayton, who found me the perfect editor . . .

Kendra Levin, whose insight into the lives of young artists brought such depth to the editorial process, and with whom it is an absolute pleasure to work . . .

All the wonderful folks at Viking/Penguin, whose talent and energy turned my manuscript into this beautiful book, especially Regina Hayes, Susan Cassel, Janet Pascal, and Kate Renner . . .

My parents, Mike and Janet Ward, who were uncomplaining chauffeurs through years of dance classes, play practices and performances, and are now a fantastic cheering squad . . .

Thomas, Mak, Sam and Jack, who told everyone that their mom was a writer long before I dared speak those words aloud myself . . .

My husband, Kevin, who makes me smile every day and is eternally on my team . . .

And my sister, Kristin, whose compassion, creativity and courage are a constant inspiration . . .

Thank you!

When you are a dancer

You learn the beginning
Is first position.

Heels together,
Feet pointed as far to the sides
As your rotating hips will allow.

And when you are small
And at that beginning,
Your body is as flexible
As your mind.

There you stand,
Potbellied,
Eager.

They do not say to you then
That, when you are sixteen,
Doubt may cramp your muscled calves,
Arch your arrow back,
Leap into your mind.

They do not say to you

When you start in first position
That you may never be

Thin enough
Strong enough
Flexible enough

That you may never be
Enough.

SARA #78

On the third of July,
I stand with a hundred other girls,
From stick-thin to gently rounded,
From tiny, taut packages of muscle
To gawky, long-limbed sylphs,
All wearing pink tights,
Black leotards.

Hair
Sprayed slick
Against our scalps,
Up and away.
Not a single stray strand to distract
From the tilt of our heads
Or the length of our necks.

I notice a few girls dared
Garnish their chignons
With beads, flowers.

Would it help them grab the attention
Of Dame Veronique de la Chance?
Of choreographer Yevgeny Yelnikov?

Of one of the other important teachers
Who have come to scout talent
Here in Boston today?
Or even catch the spectacled eye
Of the secretary in heavy, blue skirt,
Thick shoes,
Taking notes on a battered clipboard
Where our names
Are connected
To the numbers we wear pinned
Onto front and back?

I was given number 78.

Should I have worn flowers in my hair?

Sun blasts through

The giant windows
Of the ballet school in Boston,
Announcing a kinder time
Than the predawn car ride
I took to get here.

A nervous yawn builds in my throat.
I swallow it down.
Repeat with the others a series
Of tendus, pliés,
Ports de bras in center.
Then hands on barres
And me in the middle,
Neither tall nor short,
Gaunt nor round,
Certain of little more
Than that I have never danced
In a city studio before.

I learned each step I know
From Ms. Alice, the neighborhood ballet teacher,
Whose handyman husband made over
Their Darby Station, Vermont, basement

With wooden barres, wide mirrors,
Hopeful posters of satin pointe shoes
Photographed in stop-motion.

I have no way to measure
My training, my technique
Against these other girls
Until, toward the end,
Yevgeny Yelnikov nods,
Points to me.
The secretary writes something down.
An hour later, Mom, Dad, and I sit
Before a scholarship offer:
A year of study at the Jersey Ballet.

And though the July Fourth fireworks
Are still a sunset away,
My heart explodes.

In the morning, I unpin the numbers

From my leotard.
The safety pins have left little holes
In the black nylon.

I smooth the paper rectangles,
Fold them once.

I know that other girls
Were offered places at ballet schools
In better cities:

Boston, Miami, New York.

But though I did not admit this to Ms. Alice
Or Mom
Or even Dad,
I was uncertain
Number 78
Would be good enough
For any place beyond Darby Station.

Ms. Alice signed me up
For this audition,

Said I was ready.
Dad glowed with silent pride.
Mom preened, prompted, pressing
For details on what time to arrive,
Best place to park.

I nodded
As if I had dreamed of this day
Before it was suggested to me—
As if I had imagined
Dancing up Ms. Alice's basement stairs
Into some sort of real world.

Before yesterday, prima
Of small-town Vermont
Was all that I imagined.
Now
My head reels.
My dream shifts,
Expands.

Big news is

Hard to share
In a small town.

Kari, Tina, and I sit on tinny bleachers
Behind the high school,
Watch Billy Allegra drive his dad's tractor,
Plowing down waist-high weeds
From the county fairground fields
Beyond the fence.

"I'm leaving," I say, not too loud.
Watch Billy, tanned and shirtless,
Turn the tractor.
"I got a dance scholarship."

First they squeal,
Pat my back.
Then

Tina rolls her eyes.
"Least you're getting out of here."

"That's so cool," Kari says.
But her shoulder is just a little bit turned away.

My best friend, Bess, is at music camp.

I text,
"Got a scholarship
Jersey Ballet."

She texts back,
"Cool."

Then,
"When?"

Then,
"Will you be gone
Before the fair?"

For the last six summers
Tina, Kari, Bess, and I
Lolled on fence posts,
Gorged on cotton candy,
Watched older girls flirt and line dance.

Promised each other that, soon, we'd be the ones
Prancing in short-short denim,
T-shirts knotted above our waists.

Promised that, when we were sixteen, we'd dare
Sneak into the tattoo artist's trailer
To mark our friendship
In ink.

I see the penciled star
On a top September square
Of Mom's calendar by the woodstove;
Three weeks before the weekend of the fair.
Type, "Yeah. I'll be gone."

It's longer before Bess's next reply.
"2 bad."
Then a line
About a drummer,
Stephen,
She let get to second base.

When you flirt with the mirror

You never pose
In baby first position.
Nor in second,
Though they teach that next.
Feet turned out but apart
Makes for an ungainly grand plié,
A few ugly jumps.

"I am going to study
At the Jersey Ballet,"
I whisper to my reflection
In the antique looking-glass
Mom hung over my bedroom dresser.
Bat my eyes
At some invisible boy.
Imagine second base
Nothing
Like second position.

When you flirt with the mirror
You pose in fifth, arms high.
Better still, arabesque.

Best of all, not posing
But spinning in a perfect pirouette.

After the fireworks,

Summer stretches its long limbs,
An unending series of parallel days.

Mom leaves for the air-conditioned bank.
Dad races to the orchard, where the peaches
Are rosy and enticing
For a tiny window of time
Before they drop from their boughs,
Helpless fodder for deer and mice,
Splendor forgotten.

I spend long hours in my room,
Reread favorite books,
Reorganize the things I will take to Jersey,
Scribble dreams into my black-and-white notebook,
Imagine the future until I am completely terrified
Or ridiculously excited
Or weary from the humid heat.

Up the road
Mrs. Allegra can always use some help
With the newest baby
In her giant, Catholic house

Where children tumble out of crevices

Like that woman in the shoe.

I can swim in their pond
Whenever I take a handful of her school-age ones along,
Lead the girls in made-up steps
Of a water ballet and
Keep the boys from swimming out too far.

In July, Ms. Alice and her husband
Visit their grown son and grandchildren in Maine.
So I plié, relevé, stretch
Alone
In the soft sand.
Try to hold on to whatever it was
Yevgeny saw in Boston.

"Hey, Sara." Billy, the oldest,
Tosses a pinecone over my head.

We used to build sand castles on this spot
But it hasn't been the same since that night
Just after school let out
When the moon stretched Billy's shadow
Across the narrow beach.
I darted beneath a tree branch.

He met me around the scrub hedge,
My skin blushing in darkness,
His breath hotter than summer air.
He cocked his head, leaned in, but

He had grown taller,
Smelled like Dad's aftershave.

Done with sophomore year of high school,
My head level with his shoulder,
The next step should have been natural
As sun ripening fruit, but,
My mind awhirl, I felt myself pull back—
Take too many steps in the wrong direction.

He straightened up, walked away
Before the glow could fade from my cheeks.
Now I watch him from the safety of fairground fence posts.

I think of Bess and the boy, Stephen.
Wonder how she let him slide his hands
Beneath her shirt.

Pick up a pinecone
But don't throw it.

July dribbles into August

Like wet sand onto play castles,
With books and dreams of Billy Allegra
Where I am as brave
As when I wear pointe shoes.

In the evenings, Dad and I watch Mom
Make all my arrangements.
Efficient banker-mode never releases
Her hunched shoulders.
She fills out permission forms,
Piles new school supplies,
Weeds unmatched socks from my dresser drawer.

I know the suitcases I bring to Jersey
Will be packed with clothes she has chosen,
Arranged in outfits she will try to get me to wear
Even from hundreds of miles away.

One last sleepover at Bess's house,

Lying on blankets
In her basement bedroom.
Listening to her little sisters

Giggling in the hallway,
Listening to her parents

Begging them to settle down.
Listening to Bess's iPod:

Jazz
Show tunes
Big bands swinging

Songs I never hear
At the ballet studio.

Bess the trumpet player,
Room painted dare-you bright blue,
Silver-striped curtains,
Giant posters of Miles Davis, Arturo Sandoval,
Taped onto the far wall.

While I,
With my pointe shoes,
Long, straight locks,
Ballet scholarship,
Feel false,
Wishing my bedroom walls shouted in sapphire,
Wishing I liked jazz
Or Frank Sinatra,

That my sound track didn't feel
Jumbled, discordant,
Blaring from speakers outside
My heart
Or sometimes, so close
To silence.

My eyes open before Bess's

To the sound of her mom's voice
Calling down the stairs.
"Pancakes, girls?"

Pancakes at Bess's house
Are studded with blackberries,
Shreds of lemon peel,
Drowning in maple syrup
Boiled down behind their barn.

I watch Bess,
Who sleeps longer,
Doesn't crave
Her mother's creations,
Just wonders
If she wants to call Stephen
Or if she didn't like kissing him
All that much.

"Wanna go down?"
I whisper.

"Remember?" Bess says
As she opens her eyes, kicks herself free

Of the black-and-white quilt.
"We were gonna get tattoos
This fall at the fair.
A ballet slipper for you."

"A music note for you."

"Right here." Bess giggles,
Touches a spot on her breast.

"You wouldn't!"

"Where else?" She sits up.
"Where would you put that ballet slipper?"

Dad's horn outside the window
Saves me from having to pretend I know
Where I'd let the bearded guy
At the fairground tattoo parlor
Drive his pen.

"Sara! Your dad's waiting,"
Bess's mom calls.

Bess helps me roll my sleeping bag,

Collect my brush, book, mascara.

"Good-bye!
Good luck!
Have fun!"

Takes my departure for the city
As a matter of course—
Something right as a harmonic chord—
What people like us do.
Though, all the time we traded dance and music magazines,
Talked of rehearsals, recitals,
I'd secretly thought
Bess would be the one to follow a melody
Far away from Darby Station.

On the way

My heart beats faster
Every mile we drive.

Syncopated beats pound between
Excitement and
Yearning
To paste the falling brown leaves
Back on the trees,
Turn the burgeoning fall
Back to summer,
When I could loft my nose into the sun-drenched air,
Announce
My scholarship to the Jersey Ballet
Four states south
Of my country home
Without actually
Having
To go.

Turning off the exit,

Dad's fingers drum the steering wheel
Like they always do
When he doesn't have a cigarette in hand.
His car stinks of stale smoke
Despite constant attempts to quit.
Still, I can't stand
To open the windows,
The pressure in my ears, the mess of my hair,
The scary sense that something from these city streets
Will fly through the window
And hurt me.

He turns onto a wide avenue.

"Red light," I yelp.
"Shit!" Dad slams the brake.
Right hand slices across my gut.
Seat belt tightens against my neck.
His eyes telegraph a thousand apologies,
Ever afraid to mar what he sees
As flawless.

As if I could stop the forward momentum,

The ball of my foot presses
Against the car mat.

Half in the intersection,
The light still red,
I scan left and right,
Terrified an inattentive driver
Will fail to swerve around us.

At last,
Green.
Forward into the safely moving lane.

"You really want this, right?"
Dad's voice is soft as country soil.
I am not like the seasons, the seeds he knows
How to grow.

"Want what?" I taunt,
Like I would never taunt a boy my age.

A silence longer than a metronome beat.
Another.
A third.

I remember signing my name on the paper in Boston,

Mom's frantic packing.

Dad's systematic mapping of the route to Jersey
Has become my inevitable course,
So what difference would it make for me to say
That it is complicated?
That I am both excited
And afraid.

"Because you can come home anytime.
We can turn around
Right now."

Now I bleat,
"I want this."

I feel queasy
Though Dad's sudden stop
Is long past.

While my fears and wishes
Frantically duel,

Tugging my stomach and my heart
In a thousand directions,
The car drives
Straight
Toward my destination.

Señor Medrano waves

From his cement stoop.

The celebrated Chilean ballet master
Has agreed to house me for the year,
But I had not imagined
His dark, oiled hair, firm waist,
Wild eyes
Living in this bland, middle-class lane.

The split-level house, pinkish-beige,
Sits between a dozen like-painted, split-level houses.
Every fifth sidewalk square
Sports a tired-looking birch tree straggling upward
From a hole in its center.

Dad takes my big suitcase and small duffel.
I grab my ballet bag and follow him
Up the chipped stairs, through the front hall.

"So, Sah-ra."
Señor's accent makes my name all sighs.
"Here you are, *sí*?"
He leads us upstairs to my new room
With red shag carpet, smelling faintly of mildew,

A closet with sliding doors,
Twin bed with a shiny, synthetic spread
Splattered with bright poppies.

"My wife"—the teacher struggles
To find English words—
"Think you might like de flowers on de bed.
She be back next week.
When de dancing tour finish in
Vah-len-ciah." (Like Sah-ra,
All sighs.)

I am glad Señora Medrano,
The famous flamenco dancer,
Isn't here to meet me today,
Because I don't like the quilt.
But I tweak my lips up into a smile.
"Very nice."

"How 'bout we let Sara unpack a little?"
Dad says.
He and Señor
Head back downstairs.

My breath rushes out

So loud it feels like words.
I stare at the big suitcase
Beneath the one, high window.
Sit, alone
On the slippery bedspread with its giant flowers.
I am really here.
This is happening.

Tomorrow,
Will there be stairs to descend
Into the ballet school?
Will everyone know
I am the girl chosen
From the Boston audition?
Will I still be
Special enough
To stay?

After a while I go downstairs,

Steps slow,
Gaze firmly planted
On the abstract paintings along the wall.

Pretend I don't see Dad
Put his checkbook back into his breast pocket,
Señor Medrano fold the check for my room and board.
I want to be so wonderful no one would make me pay
To live in their house.

Señor pours a small cup of coffee,
Sets a tiny cookie and a spoon in the saucer.
The hot, brown smell
Comforts.
My smile becomes real.

A dark-haired boy
Saunters down the stairs.

"Julio. My son."

Flashing me a curious glance,
The boy takes a handful of cookies
From the tray.

I duck my head,
Breath quick.
Like every boy I have seen
Since June and Billy Allegra,
This one sends a curious thrill of terror
Down my spine.

Señor Medrano lets loose in Spanish phrases,
A waterfall to his
Leaky drops
Of English words.

"Yeah, Papa, I know,"
Julio returns in perfect English.

"Julio play classical guitar,"
Señor puffs.
"He need to be practicing much more
So he keep his scholarship.
Back to practicing now."
Julio helps himself to the rest of the cookies.
Turns away.

"He no work hard enough.

But he a big shot.
Does not like to practice when he can go outside,
Play basketball with friend from school.

"Sah-ra. She going to work hard
For de scholarship.
Stay here near ballet school.
Good idea."

Dad hides
Behind giant sips of coffee.

I sit, pink
And lonely.
Crumble the cookie in the saucer,
Listen to the conversation dribble
Into a vacuum of uncertainty.

In the sunshine of Boston,
It was easy to say yes
To the chance to become a real ballerina.
Now my bags lie piled
On a floor lacking hardwoods or braided rugs in dull hues,

Breathing coffee-scented air unrelieved
By the sooty comfort
Of a kitchen woodstove.

"Got to get going."

Dad jangles his keys
In his jeans pocket.
"Got a long drive."

I follow him
To the shadowy front hall.
Wetness stings the backs
Of my eyes.
I fight my rigid throat.
Release two words:
"Um, okay."

"We're proud of you, your mom and I."

"I know."

"And we love you."

"I love you, too."

Lines
Scripted,
Repeated like mantras.

Preparatory phrases
For a conversation never spoken,
A port de bras
Before
An undanced dance.

His arms encircle me.
His heart thumps into my chest
A thousand more beats
Than the syllables that escape his lips,

As afraid of conversation
As I am of boys,
Of men,
Of wind blasting through
Open car windows.

I make it upstairs

To my new room.
Close the door.

Stare at myself
In the long mirror on the wall,
Eyes still fighting tears.

"I can do this,"
I whisper.
Draw my arms up
To fifth position's gently rounded frame
Around my face.
Settle into a plié in fourth.
Push off with my back foot, though
It is difficult to spin a pirouette
On red shag carpet.

The call from Mom

Startles,
Though I knew it would come.
My cell vibrates in my pocket,
Jolts me from my stupor.

"Get there okay?"

I do not mention Dad's usual
Trouble with directions.
"Yes, Mom."

"Have you unpacked?"

The suitcase's zipper teeth
Sneer at me from the far wall.
"Pretty much."

"Had dinner yet?"

I do not wonder aloud
How I can even turn the knob,
Wrest open the door,
Enter a stranger's kitchen,
Ask for food.

"In a few minutes."

"When did Dad leave?"

"Half an hour ago
Maybe."

She talks on and on.
Asks if he smoked
Asks if he got lost
Asks if he'll make it home before dark.

I let her voice
Wash over me.
Her dissatisfaction
Is familiar.
Her anxiousness
Telegraphs through every high-pitched word,
Clicking tongue.

My eyes
Travel
To my half-opened dance bag.
Leotards and tights
Spill from the top.

Leg warmers in pink and gray
And a pair knit with red flowers
Brighten the pile.

In the hallway going up to my bedroom in Vermont
Is a black-and-white photograph
Of my great-grandmother
And her three sisters
All wearing giant, knitted hats to cover
Heads shaved by their mother
Against the rampant lice of their immigrant tenement.
Her solution
To a risk?
Remove the problem.

Was I a problem for them?
A risk to be removed?

I know I said I wanted this chance,
To dare this dream.
Yet now I wonder how
They let me go—
Whether leotards and leg warmers
Will mask my sense of abandonment.

One more week before school begins,

But classes never stop
At the Jersey Ballet.
Señor Medrano brings me at noontime.
He has a company class to teach
Long before my lesson begins
In the afternoon.

As I wait,
The company dancers
Sweat and posture
Beyond the glass window
Of the largest studio.

Across the hall, little girls
Come and go.
Their proud mothers
Smooth back their hair,
Send them into A class.

I watch them giggle,
Scurry inside,
Where a sweet-faced young teacher
Pats their heads,
Sends them to the barre.

The mothers sit just outside,
Knit, text, read magazines,
Chat about their kids,
Glance proudly
Through the viewing glass.

In the studio, I see the teacher's lips smile.
Her eyes are sharp.
Looking
For the ineffable
Something
That makes one child
A ballerina.

I am wearing leg warmers

As I sit in the hall, stretching
At two o'clock.

Inside my lunch sack,
Señor Medrano
Kindly packed
A peanut butter sandwich
Enhanced
With a slice of last night's chicken.

This bizarre concoction
Promptly finds its way into the trash,
Where I should have thrown
My pink leg warmers
When I saw the other girls come in.

At home, at the country dance school
Leg warmers
De rigueur
Fend off the New England cold
Of a drafty studio too ramshackle,
Too expensive to heat.

Here the real dancers
Bask in torpid air

Moist with sweat,
Chalky with resin and cigarette residue
Reminding me of Dad's car—
The first time the smell of cigarette
Is home.

I am wearing a pale blue leotard,
The designated shade
For my level.
An ungenerous color
That does not conceal
A single awkward angle
Or threatening curve.

In the dressing room
I watch the other girls
Trade bobby pins and tampons,
Unabashed nakedness,
And learn not to wear underpants
Under my tights.

My leotard has gauche long sleeves,
Not the chic spaghetti straps, low backs
Of the city girls.
I spot a safety pin on the floor,

Dash into a bathroom stall,
Gather the leotard front together
In little pleats.

Better?

The mirror tells me
I still look like a hick.

Their eyes are not unwelcoming,

Just curious.

A tall, thin girl with a giant blonde bun,
Lisette,
Melts into a split.

Her friend,
Bonnie,
Maybe thinner
With thick, dark eyebrows,
Bounces her knees:
A butterfly in seated first position.

Another,
Simone,
Black-haired, roundish,
Lounges on a wooden bench, talking about a boy
To a taller, redheaded girl, Madison.

These chosen girls
Are in the E class, but I
Have been told by Yevgeny
That I must begin my stay in Jersey

In C class, two levels down.
"Just to tidy up that small-town technique."

Though he has assured me that I have the talent
To leap quickly to the higher levels,
What I see now is mostly shorter, younger girls
Waiting for C class by the doorway down the hall.

While Simone and Madison,
Who look high school age, like me,

Bonnie and Lisette,
With their ballerina-straight backs,

Lounge regally outside the largest studio.

So where do I sit?

New England girls

Say "Mr."
"Ms."
Or "Mrs."
To adults and teachers.

But here,
Except Señor Medrano,
Everyone is simply, strangely
One short name.

Shannon
With cropped brown hair,
Pale skin, thin lips.

LaRae
Bright silk scarves around her head
Her neck, arms, legs unimaginably long.

Yevgeny
A greyhound, pointed nose, narrow eyes,
Froths of fine curls
Tumbling over his sharp brow.

I cannot say

These names.
Just try not to ask questions.
Nod.
Obey.

Yevgeny pats my back.
Speaks in regal, nasal tones.
"Good to see you here, Sara."

We begin technique class:
Tendus, jetés,
Pliés.

Trying to disappear,
I chose the spot at the far end of the barre.
Now, when we turn to do the left side,
There is no one in front of me
To follow.

Everyone is behind me
As I bend my knees in a deep grand plié,
Try to keep my spine pointed down, straight, remember
The things Ms. Alice taught me, the only things I know.

I can feel them judging

Even though it is my first day
And I have yet to learn the combinations
They have been taught at the Jersey Ballet
Since they were old enough to walk.

But there are no excuses
In the studio.
Yevgeny is not interested
In my story,
Only in my
Mistakes.

I brush through the layers

Of encrusted hairspray.

My hours in the studio have doubled,
Tripled
From what I danced in Vermont.

My arms ache from a thousand
Ports de bras, from pinning up a thousand chignons,
Lifting the brush,
Pulling it down.
My slick hair crackles
As I try to smooth away
The shellac
That coats my locks,
Clouds my mind.

At home, I could see clearly
Where I stood:
In the front row at Ms. Alice's studio
Where some of my dancer friends
Only came to ballet between lacrosse
And ski season, and didn't think twice
About the color of their leotards.

I knew what to do
To hold my place nearest the mirror.

Here every step
Is danced under sunless, fluorescent lights.
No open fields
In which to disappear, to pause; only, always
Mirrors
Reflecting stray wisps
Escaping from the nets and pins
No matter how much spray
I put on my hair.

How long can you go without

Talking?
I can almost count
On my bitten fingernails
And battered toes
The number of words I have said
Each day
Since I arrived in Jersey.

I could talk to Mom at night
But it hurts to call home.
I am too proud to say
That when LaRae looks at me,
Her lips are forever
Pressed in irritation,
Señor Medrano
Smiles with pity,
Yevgeny
Barks in frustration.

Madison turns triple pirouettes to left and right,
Stops without a wobble,
An expression of sheer disinterest on her face.

Bonnie's jetés jut with military precision,
Her stomach perfectly flat except
Where the bony knobs of her hips rise,
A little like Frankenstein bolts.

Lisette is a driven, dancing angel
Whose balancés and piqué turns draw a smile
Even from the eternally angry Yevgeny.

To the left, I can at best turn a solid
Double pirouette.
My tendus will never match Bonnie's
Geometric perfection.
My Vermont accent,
Inferior as my angular ports de bras,
Reveals my rural roots, basement ballet technique.

If I open my mouth,
It will only remind them
Of the imperfections of my limbs.
Silence feels safer.

"Still with Stephen?"

I text Bess.

"He's FUN.
Movies 2nite."

Her answer,
A sweet Vermont breeze
That assumes all is still wonderful with me,
Does not ask why I'm texting
Instead of stretching right now.

"Any cute boys in Jersey?"
Her question blinks.

In my class there are so many girls,
So few boys.
There are more amongst
The advanced students and apprentices,
And the company dancers,
Ethereal and mighty.

From my world apart, I watch
Fernando's perfectly sculpted arms,

Vincent's dark drama,
Remington's tall, quiet power that sometimes
Makes me wonder how Bess feels to be touched by Stephen.

Impossible to fit this reply
Into my phone's tiny screen

Even 4 Bess.

I am not sure

Whether to thank my ambitious mother
Or to curse her
For my place
At the lofty prep school
In which I have been enrolled.

A few of the other chosen girls
Go to an arts school—
Forgiving,
Undemanding,
Maybe fun.

I, instead,
Am the new junior
Amongst the wealthy, college-bound
Boys and girls
Of Upton Academy,
Who are extraordinarily well-dressed
Despite a strict dress code of burgundy
And beige.

Everywhere I turn,
There are colors I must wear on my back.

Every time I try,
I don't match the others.

Upton Academy sits

Behind an elegant row
Of green pines,
Hidden from the gritty road.
A grand oasis of
Stately walkways
Linking redbrick buildings
With heavy oak doors.

Inside, trim, modern desks,
Computer stations,
Dark, paneled libraries,
A student den with leather chairs,
Where I sit pretending not to notice

Clean-cut boys flirting
With smiling, well-dressed girls.

Pretend I don't wonder
At the thousand little conversations,
Sprinkles of laughter,
Memories of freshman and sophomore year,
The summer that just ended,
That weave into a fiber of friendship
Where I am only the fringe.

The trip from school to ballet

Is a living nightmare every day.
I stand beside the cold bus stop signpost four blocks from
Upton,
Beyond the protection of the pine-tree fence,
Where tattooed boys
Lean from the windows of motley cars,
Beckon with thick arms.
"Hey, baby . . ."

Their voices make me shake,
Long for the unpaved streets of home,
Where the route to dancing was a cleared path
Traversed by familiar faces.

The bus's arrival
Barely brings relief,
With its steps too large to climb with grace.
The other passengers glance up—
The housecoated lady with witch's eyes,
The pale young man who must be dying of something.
I sit in the open seat nearest the driver
Trying to make myself invisible.

Wait

For the bus to stop a block away
From the ballet school.

Dash across the four-lane avenue.
Run through the cracked, asphalt parking lot.
Heave open the industrial door.
Clamber down the linoleum steps
Into a cocoon
Of sweat and dreams.

Julio is at the ballet school

When I arrive.
Waiting for his father,
I guess.
I never know the plan,
Only hope someone will be there
To take me home at the end of each day.

He grins when I come in.
Walks over,
Gives my shoulder a playful push.
He is two years younger than me,
Even though dark hairs
Play across his upper lip.
My body stiffens
Against his touch.

The other girls
Beg him to play his guitar.
(He is a hopeless flirt and he does.)
Simone says I am lucky
To be a big sister in his house—
To sit at his table with Señor and Señora
And listen to talk of music and dancing every night.

But I don't feel
Like a big sister,
Only a frightened fool
And perhaps a bit above
Playing with a little boy of fourteen
Despite sometimes feeling five years old.

It is dark when we get back

To Señor Medrano's house.
But he sends Julio outside anyway
To rake their sorry scrap of front lawn
With only the pale illumination of the corner streetlight
To guide him.

I watch from the front stoop.
Wait for him to start a conversation.
I cannot tell whether he is angry at Señor's assignment,
Or at me for my coldness at the studio tonight,
But he does not try to joke or tease.

Blowing wind scatters his pile.

In Vermont, Dad rakes the leaves from the yard
Over the stone fence into the woods behind.
Here a black plastic sack waits for Julio.
I push off the chilly concrete step,
Grab at the flying leaves.
Shove dusty fistfuls into the yard bag.

Julio chuckles,
"You kind of suck at this."

"You're not so great yourself,
Mr. Classical Guitar."

He shakes the rake
Over my head.
Red and gold and brown fall flotsam
Wafts onto my oversprayed hair.

When Señora Medrano returns home
From her most recent trip
The next evening,
The yard is tidy,
The living room cleared of sheet music (courtesy of Julio),
The house vacuumed (courtesy of Señor Medrano) and
Dusted (courtesy of me).
We smile conspiratorially
Behind her scrutiny.

In class today, Yevgeny barks,

"Like Sara.
Follow Sara."

My ears blink.
I almost stop
Turning
Piqués
Like I have never turned before.

After weeks of exasperation
Something
Has connected
Between my foot
And my brain.

Each time I push off from my left leg
Onto my right toe
The box of my pointe shoe
Centers exactly.
My body lifts over it,
So secure,
So solid,
I could stand there forever.
But instead I turn

Easily,
Generously.

And again.

And again.

I reach the corner barely breathing.

Feel the eyes
Following me.

But mostly hear the magic echo
Of Yevgeny's
Hard,
Russian-accented
Shout.

"Like Sara."

Near the studio door

Apprentices and advanced students wait
For their partnering class,
Next in this space.

Today, I make my way past
Their superior clusters
With my head up

To where Señor Medrano stands,
Talking with Fernando and Remington.
I wait my turn to ask
When he'll be ready to drive me home.

"Will there be time to work on my dance?" Remington asks
Señor.
His long eyelashes beat black against his pale skin.

Señor nods.
"Remind me last half hour of class."

"Sara, you did well today,"
Yevgeny comments, passing.

Señor and the others turn their heads
As if I had just appeared
From thin air
Into an empty space.

"What time will you be finished tonight, Señor?"
I ask.

As the teacher looks at his watch,
Remington gives me a slow, curious grin.

Fondu développé

Is a melting step.
The knees of the standing leg and the working leg
Bend together, straighten together,
Until the working leg is extended in arabesque.

Feels like it should be easy.
My extension is long,
My arabesque high.

But fondu is not in the final pose,
Rather in the process,
The getting there,
With everything working together:

Learning ballet steps, trigonometry,
How to add money onto your transit card,
How to wrap a hairnet around your bun to keep it neat,
Reading so many pages of literature and history every week,
Straightening it all into some kind of manageable whole.

Fondu is not even a little bit
Simple.

Sophomore year in Darby Station,

Our English class
(Taught by Mr. Green,
Also the JV girls field hockey
And boys varsity baseball coach)
Read one single book:

Charles Dickens's *Great Expectations.*

Sitting at the desks around me,
It seemed like hardly anyone besides me and Bess
Dreamed,
Even expected
Much of anything.

Later,
After I finished the story
(Our class, in fact, never reached the end),
I saw the true irony,
Tragedy.
Felt Mr. Green was being cruel.

As if he had chosen the novel himself,
Not had it handed down to him
From the weary department head

After a quarter hour's rifling through the tattered book
stock
To see if there was a classroom set of anything
In the closet beside the library.

Mr. Green kept asking us
About the images of cobwebs
That cluttered old Miss Havisham's world
Like the distraction of green turf fields
That filled his own.

To me the cobwebs
Were less important
Than the lost love,
Lost hope,
Lost dreams
That led the spinster to
Her dusty rooms, empty, absent life,
Turning those around her cruel
By making them expect, want, too much—
The wrong things.

At my aristocratic new school,
Upton Academy,

Where no expense is spared on copies
Of anything,
A book like that
Fills barely ten days, then on to another,
Another, and
Another with
Expectations
For all.

The October trees are near naked

But my body is covered now
With hunter green,
The more forgiving leotard color
Of the next-up level
At the dance school.
And I am so delighted
That I smile at everyone.

Even the boys.

Even Remington.

He is beautiful
Tall
Strong.

The throb of my heart
Is ridiculous.
I am just sixteen and he is,
God, maybe twenty-two.
Also, he has a girlfriend,
Jane,
The company physical therapist.

I watch him from the corner of my eye
But stay near giggling Simone,
Who talks about studio gossip
And flirts with younger boys.
I would be so safe if he put his long arms around me.
His hands are so wide.

"Rem," his friends call him
(And, of course,
Jane).
"Hey, Rem!" they greet him.
Teachers and choreographers say,
"Rem, pas de chat to the left."
"Rem, partner Bonnie over there."

He is an excellent dancer
But he wants to be a teacher
And choreographer.

Can I seem old enough to like him?
The teachers say I am doing well
And allow me into some of the advanced lessons.
Still, I am officially only in D class
With mostly younger girls.
So, I try to let everyone assume I am twelve

Instead of a backwards ballerina of sixteen.

I wish I could concentrate on dancing
Instead of spending so much time pretending
I am still in junior high.
But with Rem, I want to be sixteen
Or, like Alice in Wonderland,
Sometimes smaller,
Sometimes bigger still.

Dad calls from the orchard,

Where the McIntosh apples are thick and threatening
To tumble off the trees.
He is always in a hurry this time of year
To get the harvest into cold storage
Or off to farmers' markets.
Though few besides me
Can hear the subtle urgency
In his still-soft tones.

At home, Mom will stay up late
Slicing, peeling, stirring in sugar and cinnamon.

Dad knows that Macs are my favorites
But all he says is,
"Wish you were here."

I imagine him rushing,
Supervising loaded crates,
Counting and tabulating.
It is easier to write checks for my school tuition and board
In the bounty of fall
Than it will be in winter.
So I will not be so ungrateful as to admit
That my shins ache,

That trying to keep up with city dancers is exhausting,
And that, often, I wish the same.

"I'm promoted to D level,"
I say instead.
"Green leotards and partnering classes."

I do not mention
The way looking at Rem's hands
Makes me forget
How to stand in first position,
Which I learned before I got to kindergarten.

Friday at the studio

I put my feet down tenderly.
Lightning jolts through my shins.
I try to keep my head up, move quickly,
But a pained sigh sneaks out
When my weight shifts to my left side.

"Are you feeling okay, Sara?"
Jane calls as I pass her office door.

Last night, while I waited for Señor Medrano,
I watched her kiss Remington,
Watched his endless arm sweep around her waist,
Wondered how old she was to be some kind of doctor
And if Rem likes her giant breasts.

Now, I blush.
"Um, yeah. I'm fine."

I've begun taking Partnering class,

The province of advanced students,
Where boys and girls are taught to dance
Together.

It looks so effortless when you see it happen on a stage.

"Girls must hold their own balance.
Don't make the boys work too hard, lug dead weight,"
Yevgeny commands.

Then he says to shift our weight into them.
Collaborate.
"Let them carry you.
Don't look at their hands."

How can this be?
How can you hold
Your balance and
Let them carry you?
Both, at the same time?

"Ladies and gentlemen," he says.
"Boys and girls."

Never women
And men.

Yevgeny partners me with Fernando,
On scholarship not just
Because he is a boy.
He is the best—
Arching feet,
Strong back,
A better dancer even than Remington,
Though not nearly so handsome.
Fernando's eyes never stray to my curves.
His grip is clinical, precise.

Today he will lift me into the air,
Hold my hand,
Support my back,
And make me more beautiful
Than I could ever be alone.

Saturday morning

I am early for class, as usual.
The curse of living with a teacher
Who keeps a morning schedule.

So I am there to see Remington stalk in.
Jane is five steps behind him
With a paper cup of coffee
And an irritated expression.

"Thanks for holding the door,"
She calls to his back
Before she notices me
Curled into the corner bench.

I peek at her over the top of my history book.
Our eyes barely meet
Before the blush burns my cheeks.

"Morning, Sara."
Jane flips her frown to a professional smile.
"Still limping?"

"I'm okay."

As if he had choreographed it,
We both turn our heads
To the sound of Remington dropping his dance bag
On the floor.

He gives a little bow,
Though his eyes take in only Jane as he says,
"We'll talk after class."

She sighs, glancing at me
As she puts the key in her office door.
"Sometimes Rem can be like—
A sprain.
If you're still hurting tomorrow, Sara,
I should take a look."

"Okay." I nod, astounded
At the way Jane can talk about people and pain
Out loud, in one breath.
The things I leave unspoken,
Hidden behind pallid words:

Mister . . . Ma'am . . . Please . . . Thank you . . .
Okay.

Bonnie comes early on Saturdays, too.

She gets a ride from one of her brothers
On his way to work
And has to put up with his hours.

Probably because Lisette has not arrived,
Or maybe just because she's a friendly sort,
We chat awhile.

Bonnie has ten brothers and sisters,
All older than she,
Some by decades.
And she can barely remember
All their names.

I think of Mom on the phone last night,
Asking what I had for dinner,
How things were going at school.

"Your mother feeds eleven children?" I ask,
As a picture of an enormous table fills my mind.

"We're not all still at home," Bonnie laughs,
Explaining there are only five others in the house.
She shares a room with two sisters

And the cat.
"Next year, when I start high school,
I might get my own room."

I am so grateful for her friendly conversation
I do not mention what I see.
The way she counts out raisins—only six—
To eat between afternoon technique class
And a grueling evening of variations.
The myriad trips she takes
To the dressing-room scale and
The mirror, where she turns sideways,
Wraps her stick fingers in near despair
Around her wraithlike waist.
Turns away with a fake and frozen smile
Fixed between her hollow cheeks
Above a jutting chin.

Could it be that Yevgeny's brittle gaze,
Simone's friendly teasing,
Señor Medrano's flamboyant smile,
Lisette's ceaseless perfection
Are a more intimate family?

To dance like Bonnie,
Will I have to stop craving organic apples,
The smell of a woodstove,
My mother's overprotective questions,
My father's soft, adoring gaze?

Instead embrace
Saturday mornings in the studio hallway
And eternal pliés
clutching the backs of the polished wood benches
That line the walls.

I watch Bonnie stand, stretch

Proficient, methodical, sleek.

She is grades behind me in school,
Though far wiser
In the ballet studio.

All around are
Dancers so precocious and strong,
And me pretending to be like them,
Though it can be hard to talk too long
To girls who know so much
And yet so little.

Is that why Remington,
The shadow of a beard over his chin,
Wise eyes,
Keeps drawing my stare?

Audition

Is always a scary word
Even though at the last one
I was chosen to come here.

This morning,
Bonnie and I watch Shannon
Slap a firm staple into the hallway corkboard.
Secure a single page:
Black-and-white letters,
Date and time.

Students from level B and up
Will try for parts in *The Nutcracker.*
Little girls dream of the party scene,
Older ones a chance to dance with the corps
Behind the Dew Drop Fairy,
Or perhaps be featured as an exotic candy
In the Land of Sweets.

For D and E students, and apprentices,
There is also the chance to be chosen
For a lecture-demonstration tour
Performing at schools and such
Along the eastern seaboard:

An introduction to barre exercises,
Some variations, and a story ballet.

Should I be more unsettled?
It seems to me that every day
Is an audition.

Fernando is twitchy,

Worried about the audition announcement.
All my grand ego at being his partner
Erased by the fear
That when I piqué across the floor,
Glissade and leap,
He may not catch me on his shoulder.

The posting about the audition has not left me nervous,
Only uncertain.
I will think about it tomorrow
Or maybe the next day.
Now I am pointing my toes,
Lifting my arms.

While the others around me
Stumble and slip and think about the future,
My dreams have dissolved
Into this moment
When I have to jump.

Most of the girls have been dancing here
Since they were very small.

Lisette, a miracle on legs,
Turned-up nose, giant smile
Belying the fierceness of her dedication.

Madison, casual, cool, ballerina chic,
Whose father is on the ballet board.
Half the company dancers were her babysitters.

Some days,
I partner with Fernando,
Feel LaRae pat my shoulder,
Catch a glimpse of Shannon's smile.

But more days,
I tiptoe away from Señor Medrano's disappointed shrug;
Feel the irritated pressure of Yevgeny correcting
The angle of my foot, the curve of my arm;
Chase mastery of some step, some line the other girls
    perform with ease.

Once, Mom made me watch

A PBS documentary about the prodigy Mozart,
Whose first compositions came before
He knew how to write the notes on paper.

While I watched, Mom smiled approvingly,
Encouraging my glance
Into the mirror,
Where I saw Mozart's eyes in
A girl who had danced
Since before she went to school,
Whose first memories
Were of standing in bright tutu, blue eye shadow,
new ballet slippers,
Skipping across a narrow stage.

Now, the edges of these memories sharpen.
I see the cracks in the studio floor beneath her feet,
The lack of turnout in her fifth position.

What I cannot see is answers.
Why was that blue-shadowed girl happy?
Where did she think she was going?
What did she want?

At last well turned out, on a professional stage,
Can she get anywhere so late in the game?
Where does she think she is going?
What does she want?

I should be in the studio

During the break between barre and center work,
Stretching my legs,
Working my arches.

Instead I linger in the hall
Where Remington stands
Talking to some corps dancers
About choreography.

I should be drinking water.
Instead I surreptitiously sneak
M&M's from the bag
I bought at the drugstore near the bus stop.

I should be thinking about the stripe-tied boys from Upton.
Instead I steal glances
At the wiry hairs peeking over
Rem's white T-shirt collar,
Imagine the feel of the dark stubble
Shadowing his cheeks and chin.

"Is Julio coming to the studio tonight?"

Simone stands beside me.
"Can I have some?"
She points to the candy
Tucked behind my dance bag.

I nod,
Watch her toss a giant handful
Of bright orange, red, blue, yellow
Into her mouth.

"God, I love chocolate."
She gives the slight curve of her stomach
A rueful pat.

I shrug.
Don't know if Julio is coming
Or if Simone's bright, black eyes
Have spotted any of my secrets
Less innocent than candy.

There is this tricky lift

Straight up.
The girl stands in front of the boy.
He pliés low,
Puts his thumbs together,
His palms pressing up against her thighs.
She jumps, leaning back a little,
Leveraging her straight body
To balance against the strength
Of his hands.

Today I am not with Fernando,
Who touches girls
Like vaguely disgusting objects
He is taking to the trash.

Today I am with Remington
And his hands feel different
When they slide along
The backs of my legs.

We read great books at Upton Academy,

Crime and Punishment,
Pride and Prejudice,
This and that.

In bed at night
When I can't sleep,
I think of Rodya dreaming of horses,
Sonya's pale face,
The misdirected loves of the Bennet sisters.
Wish my life were inside a book
So I could turn to the ending,
See if it is a love story
Or a gothic disaster.

At the studio,
The company dancers
Sit at the table in the corner
Littered with diet soda cans.
Some read books with corseted bosoms
And bare-chested men
Swooning across the covers.

No symbols.
No images.

Just the story of a man and his member,
A girl and her desires.
No AP literature essay required.

And then sometimes I dream myself,
Torn frock, hair flowing,
Draped across the rippling arm
Of Remington.

I should be grateful

To my school adviser,
Who arranges a ride for me
From Upton to ballet.
I no longer have to ride the city bus.

But the solution is a convertible,
No windows to close,
Driven by the giant-haired
Ruby Rappaport,
Whose father owns a restaurant chain.
The car is cherry red
With a white, collapsible roof,
Gleaming silver hubcaps.

She drives her boyfriend sometimes—
Adnan, with bronze skin
And a laid-back way of lounging in the seat.
I sit behind,
Thinking how handsome they are together.
Jealous of their easy conversation,
Barely intelligible through the windy air,
Of Ruby's slightly aggressive speed,
Open-topped along the urban thruway.

They are polite
But when they drop me
At the studio
I know they are relieved.
I cannot find the words
To reassure them
My awkward quiet is not judgment
But envy.

There's no such thing as an easy ride.

In the smallest studio

At the far end of the hall,
Remington works late

With some company dancers
Or Jane
Or alone
With an old CD player
He stops and restarts,
Measure after measure.
Stepping, standing, writing stuff down,
Scribbling it out,
His hulking hands gesture and smash.

Waiting for Señor, I watch
The shapes and patterns of making dances
Different
From just dancing them.

No school on Monday

So I will go home for the weekend,
Get back late Sunday,
Take an extra ballet class Monday
In preparation for the audition on Tuesday.

Dad meets me at the studio.
I skip Friday night's partnering class
So he won't have to drive through the city
After dark.

Ignore Yevgeny's sneer,
Accusing me of lack of dedication.

All I want is to sleep in my own bed,
A dinner without jalapeños,
The smoky heat of a woodstove,
A bright bouquet of rosy apples
Softening in the clay fruit bowl,
Filling the kitchen with their gentle scent
Of ripening off the vine.

Weekends are always too short

And most of the time is lost to sleep.

Otherwise I wear a sturdy smile,
My armor against the questions
Mom pelts from every direction, topic, side,
Spreading thick butter on homemade bread,
Sprinkling cheese onto soup.

Have you gotten taller?
Did I tell you Mrs. Allegra is having another baby?
We had a bumper crop of Jonah Golds.
Bess wants to know if you're coming to her Christmas party.

Are you happy?

Decline Ms. Alice's invitation
To join the Saturday class
In her friendly basement.

Turn down Bess's offers
Of riding to a party at Kari's
With her and Stephen.

I don't think I can bear

Sitting in the back of a car behind a boy and a girl
The way I do each day in Jersey, pretending
That I don't ache all the time,
That I'm not lonely,
That such tenderness exists for me
Outside my dreams.

Do the minimal homework.
What's the point of trying too hard
To compete against the Upton kids
With their fancy cars and private tutors?

Good enough.

Do I feel that way about ballet, too?
What's the point of staying in Jersey all weekend
For one lousy Saturday class
Where Lisette will show us all up
With her unbeatable arches
And endless energy?
Of pushing away Mom's apple pie
When I can maybe just suck in my gut a little harder?

I fend off tears the whole ride back.

At Señor Medrano's door, I wave to Dad.

"No, you go ahead.
I should get some rest.
Don't want you to get stuck
Driving in the dark."

Watch the gray Volvo
Wend cautiously away.

My parents always buy Volvos,
Safe, sturdy, crash-protected cars.
They have plenty of life insurance,
A generator in case the power goes out,
Shelves of bottled water in the garage.
They take vitamins, buy organic foods,
And their only daughter,
Who takes the vitamins along with them and still
Wants a night-light in her bedroom?
Her they drop
Three hundred miles away
On the doorstep of a stranger
To chase a dream
That exists completely
Outside

Steel car frames
Venerable insurance companies
Apples uncoated by a layer
Of shiny protection
Made from the shells
Of toxic beetles.

Inside, Julio sits,

Guitar in hand,
Sneering
At me
Or at practice
Or at life in general.

He plays a melancholy scale.

The twanging metal strings
Reverberate up my spine.

I take my bag of clean laundry upstairs.
Glance at the math textbook—

I should have read chapter four last week—

Leave it unopened on the cheap dresser.
Crawl under the slippery nylon quilt.

The Upton kids sleep in on Monday,

Maybe still in their fancy vacation houses
In the Poconos
Or on the Jersey shore.

I hit the snooze three times before
Señora's less-than-gentle tapping on my door
Reminds me I am living in someone else's house
On someone else's schedule.

Later, at the studio,
Yevgeny grabs my foot
Extended in développé a la seconde,
Squeezes my toes down hard
Toward my heel.
"Like that," he snaps,
Almost satisfied.

My glow at his attention
Darkens to a blush of inferiority.
Without his hand to force my toes,
My pointed foot reflected in the mirror
Looks weak,
Hopeless.

I hold up my chin until the end of class,
Uncertain whether I can stop it wobbling
Until Señor is ready to go home.

In the dressing room,
Bonnie drops beside me on the bench.
Rummages through her bag.
Removes an enormous pair of scissors.
"Give me your pointe shoes."

"My shoes?"

She holds out her hand.
"Last year Yevgeny said the same thing to me."

I try to forget
Mom's anxious face crunching
The long string of Upton tuition numbers,
The cost of gas to and from Jersey,
Room and board, despite the ballet scholarship,
As Bonnie rips the shank
Of my eighty-dollar pointe shoe
Away from its satin sole.

With surprising strength

Her long, thin fingers
Hack the rigid material of one sole
Across its middle,
Then tackle the other.

"Here, put them on."

I relevé.
Unencumbered by the stiff, full shank,
My mediocre arches
Bend impressively
Over the pointe shoe boxes.
In arabesque, it is easier
To mimic Yevgeny's demanding squeeze.

Bonnie giggles at my smile.

"Does everyone do this?"

"Not Lisette, of course."
Bonnie rearranges
The strand of white silk flowers
Around her bun.

I relevé in fifth, piqué,

Admire my feet in the dressing-room mirror,
Pink, curved, showy,
My silhouette more like a beach house in a grand location
Than a solid, Vermont saltbox
With its stoic lack
Of shank-bending trickery.

I am awake

Before the alarm clock
Blares into the darkness.
The audition is this afternoon.

My feet will look all new
In Bonnie's doctored pointe shoes.

I pillage through the leotards and tights
Piled on the closet floor.
Today I won't wear black—too commonplace—
Nor red—too bold.
Navy blue with a velvet bow in my hair?
Burgundy with pink flowers?

Does it matter there's a tiny hole
Where I've gathered the front of the burgundy leotard
With a safety pin?
Does it matter the navy is a little stretched out in the seat?
Will it make any difference?
And if they don't choose me,
Can I pretend that I don't care?

The floors of the ballet studio

Are sticky with resin.
The mirrored walls so peppered with fingerprints
Reflections look like those impressionist paintings
Made from tiny dots.
Every conversation is underscored
By the accompanists' plonking piano notes
As if we are all
Always
Onstage.

"Do you have an extra hairnet, Sara?"
Simone fidgets on the bench beside me.

"Sure." I rummage through my bag.
Her hair is black and mine is brown.
The net won't match
But such things trouble Simone no more
Than carrying on a half hour's conversation
Wearing only a pair of tights.

I need to breathe,
Push out the fear
With the perfect, driving burn of my hamstrings
When my thighs first kiss the floor.

They call me
Into Studio C with Simone and Lisette,
Bonnie and Madison.
We are auditioning for a pas de deux so . . . Yes!
Remington is here.

And my eyes are so stuck
On his broad back
I almost do not hear them tell me,
"Double pirouette, Sara."

From fourth position
I push my heel against the floor,
Snap my head around,
Open my arms to catch the sunlight
Coming through the side window,
Reach for something . . .

For him.

Everyone is relieved

When it is over.
Draped across the hallway benches,
Lingering awhile before returning
To the locker rooms
To change back from ballerinas
To ordinary girls.

"What did they tell you?" Simone asks.
They said very little, so I just go,
"Could you believe Fernando?"

Bonnie says, "He sure loves his own face!"

I laugh along.
Pretend I don't notice Remington
Come back through the door,
An absent-looking smile on his face,
Cigarette dangling from his fingers.
The aroma is chalky, dirty, metallic.
I know it is bad
But I like it.

Simone waves him over
But he sits beside me,

His arm dropping along the back of the bench.
Small talk about the audition combinations,
How Yevgeny is a taskmaster.
"But a great teacher.
Don't you think, Sara?"

Rem sounds so casual I can't figure
Whether all he's thinking about is the audition
Or if some part of him feels the blood
Pulsing through my skin where his wrist touches my
    shoulder,
The way every other part of me is straining to be
The forearm his fingertips are absently stroking.

Has he been feeling my eyes on his back?
Sensing me hovering near him?

Madison and Simone can't join him and his friends
For pizza at Denardio's tonight.

And me?

"Where's Jane?" escapes from my stupid lips.

"She's in Ohio. A family reunion."

I will myself to hear disapproval in his tone,
Feel my head nod yes.

I do not know what I am doing,
Only that I want to go with him.
Stand up.
Leave my fears, my sense
In the sticky dust
Of the studio floor.

For once I don't hesitate to undress

In the locker room.
Tear down the bun.
Add some lip gloss.
Ditch the baby-doll dress for jeans
And the scoop-necked black jersey
That shrunk in the wash.

I am already by the door when Rem shows up
With two more grown-ups—corps dancers.
Paul has a car.
Don sits in front,
Criticizes his driving in a strident yet tender way.
Rem jokes with them and doesn't seem to mind
I have too little breath to speak.

At Denardio's I sit beside him,

Lifting pizza to my mouth
For minute bites,
Feeling ensnared in the red vinyl booth,
A half-acknowledged warning that I shouldn't have come
Without any other girls.

"So we're back into *Nutcracker* season,"
Paul sighs.

"Again." Rem nods.
"Not much time for my new piece."

"The one you work on in the little studio?"
I wipe my greasy fingers on a brown paper napkin.

"You watch me, Sara?"
Rem's smile starts in the left corner
Of his mouth.

I swallow hard,
Saved from answering by Paul and Don,
Who wave to some friends by the bar
At which I am too young to sit.
"We'll be back in a minute."

"Sure." Rem inspects the rim of his mug.
I stare at the empty seats across from us
But imagine Rem's arm unraveling from Jane's waist,
Sweeping a gallant greeting to the little studio mirror.

Under the table
Rem drops his wide palm
Over my knee.

I mask my sharp inhale with babble
About the fouettés in *Le Corsaire*,
The audition, tour dates.
But they are not words,
Just the obligatory sounds of an accompanist's piano chords
Clanging and echoing in the dark tunnel
Between my ear and my brain—
They tumble from my mouth like marbles,
Round and meaningless.
All that makes sense is to feel
The heat of his palm
Burning through my jeans.

"It's fun partnering with you."
His face comes close, grinning

Before he brings his lips to mine.

Sometimes the earth shifts beneath your feet
Like jumping on a hill of sand.
What was true and solid begins to slide, dissolve.
Your thoughts unravel faster than a satin ribbon
Whose edge hasn't been burned
Until you sit amidst a tangle of limp, pink threads,
Unable to reason
At all.

There is an uncomfortable silence

Across the table.
My eyes flash open for a second to see
Paul and Don return to our booth.
Their expressions seem to telegraph one syllable:
Jane.
Jane!

I remember her offer
To look at my sore legs
With a millisecond of guilt
But

Rem's head is turned,
Kissing me.
His lips are too soft,
Too wet.
But I have never been kissed before
So maybe this is how it is:
Hungry mouth devouring my face,
Hands dangerous.

I close my eyes again.

How do nights like this end?

Can I ask him that
As the pizza cheese congeals
And the condensation drips
From the outside of forgotten drinking glasses?

"Hey, we're heading out.
Early rehearsal tomorrow."
Paul takes out his wallet,
Looks at the check.

Rem pulls his hands away,
His expression unreadable, bland.
"How'd it get so late?
We should get you home."

I stand up,
Follow Don
To the flashing neon exit sign.

"How about you sit up front, Sara,
So you can show Paul
Where you live."

"Don't you know where Señor Medrano . . . ?"

I start,
But Rem and Don are already
In the back,
Paul's lips are pursed,
The engine is humming.

Outside Señor Medrano's

Rem doesn't get out
Or offer to walk me up
The crumbling stairs.

I watch Paul pull away from the curb,
Try to recount the number of beers
Rem drank.

Is this what a first kiss is supposed to be?
Disapproving eyes, probing hands, curious guilt,
A lonely walk to the door.

Señor Medrano's front hall is icy from open windows
Battling the acrid smell
Of something recently burned in the kitchen.

I wonder at the raw tenderness of my lips
And whether Remington will still like
Partnering with me
Tomorrow.

Another kind of dancing

Is the Fall Formal
At Upton Academy,
Which has become the obsession
Of Katia and Anne
And the few other girls I've gotten to know
In the little time I spend at the school
Before rushing to the studio,
Missing every sport, club, casual gathering,
Missing everything that high school
Really is.

At Upton I am a wave
Passing through—
A shadow that will not be missed
If I turn up late or leave too early.

I do not even care
About the stupid theme,
Arabian Nights,
Nor the dresses
Nor the rented limousines
Until Barry comes to me at break
Before history. He leans against my locker,

A flush creeping up to his narrow blue eyes,
Tugs at his regulation tie
As if it's strangling him.

Barry asks if I know whether anyone's asked Katia
To the dance.

The question is odd
Since Katia is not my close friend.
And if he had really wanted to know
He should have asked Anne.
But I stupidly say I'll find out
And he agrees to call me after school.

Ruby Rappaport's car is in the shop

So I ride the evil bus down Harris Avenue,
Heart pounding,
Unusually distracted.

By the time the bus arrives
At the studio,
I have decided Barry was trying
To ask *me* to the dance
And that I should suggest we go together
When he calls.

I cannot sit still.
Pace the studio halls
Trying to forget
The tantalizing electricity of Rem's lips,
The disapproval in Don's stare,
The urgent knot in my stomach,
Until my cell rings
Three minutes before class.

I slide into a corner.
"Hey, Barry."

“Hey, Sara.
I guess I don’t need any help.
I asked Katia.
She said yes.”

My stupid heart
Drops into my worn ballet slippers.

My face burns.
Ears ring.

I stumble into the studio
Even though, until four hours ago,
I had not stopped dancing long enough to reflect
On fall formals, Arabian Nights,
The kind of music ordinary teenagers move to,
Or whether any of it is made
Of violins, violas, twinkling pianos
That are an easy fit
For ports de bras
And pliés.

After class, Jane is sitting on Rem's lap

But he gives me a curious look over her shoulder.

My insides clutch,
Remembering
His hands under the table.

I cannot figure
Whether I care
About Barry's rejection,
About Jane's fingers
Twirling through Rem's straight hair,
About Upton Academy,
Or ballet,
Or anything at all.

We cluster around the bulletin board

Where Shannon has posted the cast lists.
I have the part of Mama Bear
In the "Goldilocks" Tour.

But all I can think about
Is my role as a Snowflake
In *The Nutcracker*,
Which will mean I cannot go home
For Christmas.

That's enough to stop me eating.

Well, not completely.
I eat dry toast at breakfast time,
Ignoring the strange bean-based meals
And stinking cups of *maté*
Señora and Julio enjoy.

At lunch there is the salad bar at Upton:
Grapefruit sections, lettuce,
And sometimes a cookie.
I have little self-control
And I hate myself for that.

I am not hungry anymore,
Though I crave chocolate, sweets, love.
I am numb to the days as they pass;
Their numbers no longer lead to my escape
Back to Vermont.
And there are rehearsals all the time.

For another thing,
It turns out Rem is my Papa Bear,
Which feels more dangerous than dessert.

In Ruby's car after school

My cell rings.
Mom's voice is garbled
By the shearing wind.

Ruby says
She will not close
The convertible's roof
Unless there's an inch of snow at her feet.

On the awful bus yesterday
Before Barry called,
I had texted Mom,
"I might need
A new dress."

Now, regretting typing every letter,
I shout my pat replies
About breakfast, lunch, dinner,
Dreams.
Pretend I don't hear questions
I cannot answer.

Mom has not come to Jersey to see me.
Says her bank schedule keeps her in Vermont.

Perhaps she has begun to enjoy
Parenting from a distance,
Clean and sanitary
Without visible tears.

Bess is going to the Darby Days dance

With Stephen, who has been her boyfriend
For a record-breaking three months.

I don't tell her about Barry and the Fall Formal,
Or ask who Billy Allegra is taking,
Or for her advice on stolen kisses from an older boy,
A man.

Text back,
"Too many rehearsals.
Have 2 skip Upton fall dance."

Just a safe, painless,
Nine-word
Lie
I try to believe myself.

My head feels light as my leg

As I push through ronds de jambe
That circle endlessly back to front,
Reminding me my stomach
Has nothing to ponder.
My leg has nowhere to go
But back where it started.

Rond de jambe
Muddles me.
Don't see a way
To make it beautiful,
Much less perfect
Or even finished.

Upton, ballet
Billy, Barry
Rem, Rem
Remington

Round and round
And round and
Round.

Allegro,

As in its essential counterpart,
Music,
In dance means fast,
Movements quick, precise.

Rehearsal life is all allegro, rushing
From studio to studio,
From practicing the tour lecture–demo and story ballet
To learning the opening steps for *The Nutcracker*
Snowflakes
And then back to classes.

In Variations, we are learning to dance
Aurora's Act III solo,
Where the cursed Sleeping Beauty
Awakens to

A handsome prince,
A perfect marriage
And, despite her century of sleep,
Performs a virtuosic dance

That I can only stumble through, regular sleep cycle
notwithstanding.

My part in the tour is easy.

Mama Bear wears a costume, padded fat.
I do not even wear pointe shoes.
They are the province of everyone's favorite,
Lisette.

I plié and pas de basque,
Gambol and fake stumble
While Goldilocks Lisette
Pirouettes and flutters
In her charming pas de deux
With Fernando
The woodsman
(Not in the original tale).

But in the bus
On the way to the auditoriums,
Janeless Rem sits with me in the back.
Tells me about making dances
Or tucks an earbud into my ear to share
Some new, strange piece of music I imagine
Bess would understand.

And sometimes,
On the long rides home,

I fall asleep
With my head on his shoulder.

Thanksgiving is about food,

Which is complicated,
But not so much for me
As for Lisette and Bonnie,
Whose bones nearly poke through their skin,
Whose periods never come.

I am naturally thin enough,
Too lonely and bored
For fasting.

My diets are more distraction
Than discipline.
I'll try any fad—
Boiled eggs,
Lemon water,
Lettuce and tuna—
For the chance to talk about it
With the other girls,
To belong,
If only in my abstinence
From food.

Dad is driving me home the day before
Thanksgiving

And back Thanksgiving night.
Too many rehearsals for more.

I will go north,

Stuff myself with apples with onions,
Mom's cautiously overcooked turkey,

Sleep restlessly with the knowledge that Rem
Is going to Jane's uncle's house
In Pennsylvania.

It feels like I am always returning

From my brief escapes to the country,
Where I try to remember the dreams
That stole me away
From my cozy four-poster,
Pastel-colored quilt,
Couches peppered with contented cats.

Try to forgive

My friends at home
For their prom dates and sleepovers and regular lives,

Myself
For my troubling ambitions in a distant city,

My parents
For letting me go.

At Upton, Katia shows me pictures:

The Fall Formal,
The gym draped in gauzy Arabian scarves,
Barry in a ridiculous blue tux.
I tell myself I am glad

To have missed standing beside that clown.
I am an artist
Untroubled
By childish high school affairs.

I do not say to Katia
That Barry kind of asked me first,
Because I do not want to tell myself
About another kind of rejection.

I have this fantasy

Where I am a famous ballerina
And my picture
Is displayed on the cover
Of a thousand magazines.

All the coolest kids at Upton regret
Not noticing the shadowy ballerina
Dancing through their halls.
Try to be my friends.

Remington confesses his true love.
Swears he only stayed a little with Jane
Because I was so young.
He was waiting for me.

In my fantasy I never
Actually
Dance.

Jane looks depressed,

Sitting with a cluster
Of company ballerinas.

Marie, whose legs cross and uncross,
Tipping her cigarette ash
Into a soda can
With ethereal grace.

Galina, with her romance novel
Title in gold letters,
Volume fatter
Than her waist.

I think of my tattered copy
Of *The Thorn Birds*,
Stolen from my grandmother's hall bath
Last summer.
The way those chapters
Make my breath come fast—
Make me want
Some unspeakable thing.

Do such books
Agitate

These queens of the ballet,
Make them come undone inside
The way that one does me?
But it can't be so,
The way they flick that ash without a quiver.
Or is it just that their training,
The great, technical control
They have over their bodies
Protects them even
From wanting?

In the locker room I hear

Why Jane is so upset.

Simone always spews gossip
While she pins up her hair.

At Thanksgiving Rem told Jane
There was another girl.

My heart stops,
Wondering
If the girl
Is me.

Simone knows all the crushes

And even I cannot miss
Her incessant queries
About Julio.

Last week, she stood beside me, watching
My face as much as
Rem dancing
In the small studio.

I am light with hope

At the brushup rehearsal for "Goldilocks."
I try to feel a difference
In Rem's palm
As it guides my elbow.

He escorts me, waddling
To our mock breakfast table
Where we pretend to be disgusted
By overheated porridge.

His brown eyes twinkle.
They always do.
He pushes his straight bangs
Off to the side,
Smiles a silly Papa Bear smile
That makes me want to dive into his giant arms.

He is too tall to be a star dancer
But so expressive, smart.

Rem occupies a curious space
Between student and teacher.
A man, yet, as a choreographer,
Something of a prodigy.

Are we alike
In that in-betweenness?
Can he see,
When I smile my blue eyes back
At his brown ones,
The country-city-woman-girl
Dancer, student
Bewildered
Unbelonging
Yearning?

Do I dare ask him about
Catcher in the Rye
Daisy Miller
The Great Gatsby?

Do I dare ask him for what I want,
As if I knew it,
Could find it on some page
In some chapter
In some book?

Rem and I lean against the barre

While Lisette does her "Goldilocks" solo.

She piqués, relevés, and the music follows her,
Playing a game of follow-the-leader
As if they could take turns
As if the music sees her step and twirl
As if she knows every tune before
It leaves the piano keys.

It would be easier
If I could hate her.
Perhaps I should,
As I watch through the glass
Where she practices
Alone
Before and after
The teacher and the rest of us
Fill the room
With our lesserness.

Is she trying
To make it hard
For all us others

To scurry in the shadow
Of her dedication?

Yet there is sweetness
Behind those driven eyes.
Ballet
Is her one and only
Uncomplicated lover,
Best friend.

We begin the bears' feature.

Remington's fingertips
Trace the stiff ridges of my forearms,
Meet my palms.

Simone, the Baby Bear,
Ducks beneath the bridge
Of our joined hands.

Can she see my hair stand on end?
Does everyone notice my fleeting glances toward the
window
Where I am always checking for Jane?

Rem is like chocolate,
Making me feel hungry and guilty
Always and at the same time.

Would it help if I told him
I am all of sixteen?
Though I try not to mention this
At the studio.

Sixteen is
Wanting.

Battered toes, aching shins.
Hope for the growing strength of my arches.
Curious despair at the curve of my breasts.

Sour not sweet.

They hand out the paperwork

After rehearsal.
The fall tour will finish with a three-day trip
To schools in northern Jersey
And a stop for a dance class
In New York City.

After that
Our lives are in the clutches of *The Nutcracker*,
The bread-and-butter of the ballet economy,
The chance for us students
To dance with the company
On a giant stage.

I read the trip itinerary,
Pushing beans and shreds of meat
Around the jade-green dinner plate.

Julio taps my shoulder.
"Want to play cards?"
Our tentative friendship has begun to grow,
Maybe because my lust for Rem
Has made it easier to be in the house
With this other boy.

I show him the paperwork, the permission slip.
"Who should sign this?"

"Is Rem going?"
He asks right away.

My eyes shoot down to the ace of spades.

He laughs. "Simone has a big mouth."

"Does that make her a good kisser?"
I am surprised at my boldness.

Julio's ears turn red.
He laughs but
Tosses the deck of cards
A little too roughly my way.
"Nosy!"

"You started it!"
I won't tell him
About Papa Bear.

"Just give the form to my dad.
He'll sign it."

Like a million times before,
I realize how free I have become
Since being dropped off
At Señor Medrano's doorstep.

The first school on the tour is a dump

With a floor like cinder blocks.
Every step hurts my shins.

After the performance-opening demonstration
Of ballet barre exercises,
I rush back to the dressing room
To change into Mama Bear.

Peel off my leotard.

As I turn to look for some Tiger Balm
To relieve the ache of my legs,
I see Rem staring
At my topless body
Through the gap in the makeshift dressing-room curtain.

And I hesitate
Before I wrap my arms around my chest.

Afterwards, riding the bus to the motel,

Rem guides me to the last row.
Concealed by the seat back
He draws me close,
Reminds my lips
Of his kisses,
Does things that make my tights damp between the legs.

The chaperones are strict,

Assigning us girls
Four to a hotel room,

Where everyone doses up on Advil
To beat back the pain
Of the unforgiving floors.

The room stinks of Bengay,
Lisette's leotard
Rinsed and drying on the towel bar.

On television
Old men tell jokes behind desks.

In the bathroom, Bonnie
Vomits again.

Beneath the covers
My body aches
For Remington.

On the last day of the trip,

As we are leaving the studio
Of the city ballet company
Where we took a grueling class,
Rem says in the most offhand way,
"I'm staying with friends in the city tonight."

My mind does a quick calculation.
Bonnie sits with Lisette,
Madison with Simone,
Fernando with no one,
Staring out the window
Or perhaps at his own reflection
In the fingerprinted pane.

I curl up alone in the seat.
The bus swerves cruelly
Around sharp curves,
Lurches
Over potholes.
My stomach revolts.
My body misses
The comfort of wrapping fingers,
The distraction of kisses.

Back at the studio

I watch Jane
Work with company dancers and students.
Her face, friendly and professional,
Does not look like she is lost, missing a piece
Of something. Her heart must be fine
And I comfort myself, recalling that morning
Not long ago
When Rem stalked into the studio
Leaving her in the doorway's shadow.

The tape measure

Is unforgiving:
My legs are shorter than Lisette's,
My waist thicker than Bonnie's.
The *Nutcracker* costume mistress pushes me this way and that.
I try on a shimmering white unitard, a sash of gray chiffon,
A tight silver cap.

He hasn't come back to the studio yet.

I sit with the other girls in the hall,
Sewing ribbons on my new pointe shoes.

Every time someone comes through the door
I jump.

Is Simone watching?
Can Madison see my desperation?

My mind travels to a horrible place
Where he has simply disappeared.
No one knows what has happened.
And I am left here
Alone.

The second hand rond de jambes
Around the clock.
Rehearsal begins in nine minutes.

One slipper sewn.
One bloody finger prick
Dotting red-brown spots
On the pink satin ribbon.

I put my finger in my mouth.
Suck off the dirty blood.
Start on the other shoe,
Though there's little chance
I will be finished in nine minutes.

At eight minutes
He swoops through the door,
Face shadowy with unshorn beard,
Coat bundled over his arm.

"Friend's car broke down on the highway,"
He says to no one in particular.

Dashes toward the costume shop.

I wait for his gaze
To rest specially on my face
But there is nothing.

Am I lonelier now
Than when my sad imagination
Had him disappear?
Heart torn,
Loosing tiny droplets
Of sorrow
No tape can measure
No needle can mend.

Señor Medrano puts me in the front row

To learn the steps for the Snowflake ballet.
They are not very difficult;
What is hard is matching with the other girls,
Counting out the music exactly right.

My toes push down on the hard floor,
Nearly unprotected
By the worn boxes of my old pointe shoes—
The price for failing to finish
Sewing the new ribbons.

But Señor smiles, encouraging.
The music carries me
As I lead my line,
Glance up at my fingertips
In a glorious port de bras,
Loneliness, for the moment,
Forgotten.

At Upton it is all about

The PSAT score reports that have come in.
Katia and Anne are planning a trip
To visit colleges along the Atlantic coast.

I stare at the envelope
From the College Board.

"Open it."
Anne laughs
Her superior laugh.
The intellectual
With the well-cut
Ralph Lauren
Burgundy jacket
That nods to Upton's dress-code standard
Without seeming uniform at all.

I slide my finger under the flap
Pull out the thin, computer-generated page
Read and pass it over.

I barely remember taking the test in October.
Can't think if anyone told me it was happening
Until that day.

Had to borrow a pencil
To fill in the monotonous ovals
That made me late to ballet class.

Yet, even in my disinterest,
I can see the very high percentile marks
That draw the smile
Off of Anne's lips,
Make Katia's pale eyes bulge.

"So what colleges are you thinking of?"
Anne asks.

"I haven't really thought about college,"
I confess.

And we can be friends again.

Could it be that high PSATs make me lighter?

Because I can barely remember the windy ride
Down Harris Avenue,
Do not even celebrate
Ruby Rappaport's fight with Adnan,
Which means I sit in the front seat.

My poker hair does not resist
Being twisted into the bun.
I do not feel hungry,
Despite a lunch of six orange wedges.
The dark green leotard
Slides over my stomach
Like silk.

I choose the far end of the barre
But, unlike the first day,
I know the routines.
My back held straight,
Arms taut but graceful,
Clenching my feet into perfect arches.

After the barre, ballet class moves to center,

The pretend, practice stage
Where we tendu, plié, jeté
All over again.
But this time, we dance for our mirror audience,
Posing coquettishly in effacé,
Twisting and angling,
Morphing from student to performer
For forty-five minutes or an hour.

Inside my new pointe shoes,
A bleeding blister
Burns delightfully
Through a grueling adagio combination:
Arabesque into an epic promenade
That somehow does not cause a cramp in my thigh.
Then an allegro: sauté, chassé, piqué turns.

I hover over myself
Watching.
Mind and body separated,
Each in control
As though there are two puppeteers
Working the strings of my marionette self.

Perfection.
I even feel the muscles of my face
Draw my lips
Up into a smile.

Ballerinas are often compared to butterflies.

I understand today
As I flit across the black floor,
Feel Simone's eyes on my back,
A dark brown version of Katia's gaze,
As if jealousy begets more jealousy,
Perfection more perfection.

We come to révérence,
A curtsy to thank Señor Medrano
For teaching our class.
The piano smacks its final chord.
Silence shatters the magic.

Señor pauses in the doorway to speak to a parent.
Students drop to the floor, pack up shoes and gear.

Remington steps into the room.

Behind him
No sign of Jane
But I watch his careful eyes
On Señor's back.
Señor gives the classroom

A curt farewell nod,
Strides out
On character shoes,
Soft and black.

Chatter rises.
Rem saunters over,
Slides onto the floor beside me.

"Whatcha been up to?"
As if I had not been counting every hour
Since his last touch,
Calculating the depth
Of his rejection.

Twenty minutes 'til the next class

And all around us
Dancers trickle in and out.
I sit immobilized,
Pointe shoes half untied.
Remington launches into
Words.

I watch his lips move,
Hands gesture.
The dark brown hair on his forearms lifts
As he swings through a giant
Port de bras

Describing some dance he is making.

He picks up my hand,
Draws me to standing,
Demonstrates a parallel promenade.

I try to imitate,
Satin shoe ribbons trailing behind me on the floor.

"No. No. Like this, ballerina."
His chuckling words waft through

The smoke in my ears.
I let him show me
Steps I have not seen in ordinary classes,
His expression all fire
As he shares his pas de deux.

He releases my fingers
That weep for his touch.
I look down.

My feet are still in parallel,
Trying to make
The stylized, geometric
Steps
Of Remington's ballet.

"Nice."
His voice approving, low,
Inviting.

What does he want?

What do I want?

Remington leans against the barre,

Looking at me
As the clock ticks toward Variations.
I cannot read the expression in his eyes.

The studio begins to fill.

Bonnie and Madison drop onto the floor beside me.

"We're going to the movies tonight,"
Bonnie says.
"Wanna come?"

"What movie?"
My voice shatters the fine glass air
Between Remington and me.
I see him, through the spiderweb cracks,
Turn away.

"We'll figure out what's starting
After we get to the mall.
My dad's gonna drive."
Madison looks at me.

"Sounds like fun,"
I manage.
Push my voice into air
That still snaps.

"Cool." Bonnie stands up,
Heads for the rosin box near the door
To coat her pointe shoes
Against slipping.

"So, we'll meet up after Variations."
Madison follows Bonnie.

Remington leans away from the barre,
Gives his back a casual stretch.
"I can give you a ride
To the movies."

I focus my energy on wrapping the retied end of my pointe
shoe ribbon
Under the knot. Thoughts and feelings jumble
While my heart hiccups, my breath sticks in my chest.
"Okay."

In Variations class,

We are working on *Sleeping Beauty*,
Much more formal, familiar
Than the forward-toed, eclectic gait
Of Remington's promenade.

Aurora, the Sleeping Beauty,
Is supposed to be sixteen, like me.
Her dance, light with anticipation of all that is to come,
Giddy with childish glee
At her birthday celebration.

I love the gentle build
Of Tchaikovsky's music.
Joyful, precise développés en tournant
That explode into a line of piqué turns,
Tough and spectacular.

Every girl dreams of performing them—
Lisette and Bonnie, Simone and Madison—
All of us tendu and spin
Again and again.

This will be the last Variations class
Until *The Nutcracker* is over.

A long time to remember
Even delightful steps
To delicate music.
I try to drive them into my muscles
Beside the incessant ache
Of yearning.

"Tonight, Madison, Bonnie, and I
Are going to the movies."

I tell this to Señor Medrano.
Try to keep my eyes casual
Like I do not really care
Who else is going out tonight.
Or that I will get a ride with Remington.

Señor smiles, pats my head
Like I'm a little girl.
I watch him push through the metal door,
Disappear from the studio.
Turn back to the strange adventure,
Uncertain bed
I have made for myself.

Madison's dad comes

For her and Bonnie.
"You sure you don't need a ride?"
Madison heaves her chic, black, quilted ballet bag
Over her shoulder.

I look at the solid, suited man
Standing in the doorway,
Poking at his cell phone,
Tapping his foot.
I imagine his car's thick, safe metal,
Airbags,
Clean, leather seats.

From the corner of my eye,
I see Remington
Joking with Paul and Don.
He nods at me.

"I've got a ride. I'll meet you there.
Text me the movie you pick."

I ride on the back of Rem's motorcycle.

Try to forget my fear
Of the wind
Turning my sleek braid
Into a messy ponytail
Set behind a frazzled halo
Of escaped brown strands.

". . . if we make a quick stop at a party?"
He hollers into the wind.
In answer, I can only squeeze him tighter.

Rem turns up a narrow road,
Stops at a house as big as mine in Vermont.
Dark wood and stucco decorate the front.
A dusty chandelier lights the grand entry hall
Bedecked with a tattered Persian rug.
Bamboo shades slant over the windows.

Rem saunters through a crowd of faces
To a kitchen with dingy tile floors,
A glass-and-iron table with mismatched chairs,
A dark gold refrigerator.

He takes out a beer,

Lights a cigarette,
Deftly twists the flame toward his palm,
Offers it to me, saying,
"You shouldn't smoke."

I take the thing.
Hold it in my hand a while.
Hope that I look sophisticated.
Remember the myriad cancer threats
Spoken like mantras by Mom to Dad,
A constant refrain of my childhood.
Draw the smoking tumor to my lips.
Hold it there long enough to look courageous.
Satisfy myself by striking a studied pose,
Left arm across waist
Right elbow balanced on left knuckles
Right palm up, cigarette pointed coolly,
Safely
Away.

The party is crowded.
Rem nods at people,
Taps his foot to the pulse of the room.
The music is loud.
Ballerinas look all wrong

Bouncing and thrusting
To beats driven by drums
Instead of the sweeping bows of violins.

I think of Variations class
Just hours ago,
Safe under the eyes of Yevgeny and Señor Medrano
Trying to meld my body
To Tchaikovsky's lilting tune.
I could not hear the music quite right,
Felt like Señor wanted me to take the first step
A moment before each measure began.
Felt my solid, even strong, fouetté turns end
Always a moment too late.

Now I resist
Spinning a circle of fouettés
To try to see if I could do them
To this music,
So loud it pounds into my gut.
How could I fail to follow?

The snaking cigarette ash
Threatens
To fall onto the carpet.

I wander,
Open a door looking for the bathroom—
A place to flush away the cigarette,
Try to repair my ravaged tresses—
Only to find a bedroom,
Paul and Don
Kissing.

I am jealous of the dance they do.
Steps already learned.
Timing right.
No test to pass.
Audition over.

With Remington
I am back at the studio in Boston—
Sun glinting sharp
Against giant mirrors,
Turning my reflection
To a harsh, uncertain glare—
Wondering how I came to this place.
If Remington has given Jane's part
To me.

Rem's giant palm

Cupping the back of my neck
Erases my fleeting urge
To remind him of my plans.

"Still wanna see a movie?"
He surprises me.

I nod, grateful.
Pull my phone from my pocket.
Bonnie has texted
A time and title.

"We'll have to hurry."

"Why?"
Rem swirls his denim jacket
Around his shoulders,
Pushes his arms through both sleeves
In one gesture.

"The movie starts in ten minutes."
I hold up the phone.

"Not at the mall." He laughs.

"Let's stay here, okay?
So we can talk."
His fingers walk
Down the knobs of my spine.

I follow him.
To a giant porch sprawled across the back of the house.
Along one side, a yellow sheet hangs—
A makeshift movie screen.

People loll on wicker chaises
Wrapped in blankets.
The laughter gets loud.

Rem draws me down
To an oversized wooden chair
A little bit behind the group,
Which does not stop someone
From passing back a joint
Nor Rem from inhaling deep,
Right arm across my shoulders,
Hand dangling over my breast.

He offers it to me
But I shake my head,

Watching
For the inevitable policeman
To catch us all,
To change me from good girl to bad.
I have no idea what is playing on the screen.

“R U coming?”

Bonnie texts.

“Can’t get there in time,”
I send back.

Put the phone on vibrate,
In my pocket,

Away.

Even without smoking,

My head grows cloudy
From the waves of sweet-smelling smoke all around.

Rem gives me a silly grin,
Rolls his head back.
His straight brown hair
Makes half a halo over his eyes.
Grabs my thighs with big, hot paws.

"You're so beautiful," he mumbles.

Now I hear the music

Scratching through dusty speakers
Beside the back door.
I was never very tuneful,
Don't have Lisette's lyrical ear.

I choke down dry mouthfuls
Of salty, yellow popcorn.
Rem's words sink slowly
Into my addled brain.
Beautiful?

Wish for Paul and Don
With their tender domesticity
To take me home,
Because here there is chaos
Inside and outside my mind.

On the screen a vampire
In black and white,
A screaming girl
In stiff satin.
I dive into Rem's hungry arms,
Let his sliding fingers
Bury all my fears.

When the credits roll
I am drunk with touch and kisses.

"Take me home,"
I whisper.

Rem steers me quickly past clumps of people,
Cluttered furniture,
Out the door.

On the motorcycle behind him,
Arms wrapped around his muscled waist,
I am not certain to what home Rem thought
I had asked to be delivered.

Rem's apartment is three flights up,

The paint in the hallway
Chipped and grim.

He bounds up the stairs,
Holding my hand.

My other hand fingers
The cell phone in my pocket.
Should I call Señor Medrano?
And what would I say
If he answered the phone?

“What is it, Sara?”

He is all quiet concern
As I hesitate in his doorway.

I look round at the art museum posters
Thumbtacked to the walls,
The couch draped with a tie-dyed blanket,
Two wooden armchairs with orange seats.
All so much more inviting
Than slippery poppies
And damp-smelling rug.

“Why were you so cold to me
Before class today?”
Maybe the lingering pot
Has made me brave.

He grimaces, then grins.
“Do you think Señor would approve?
I’m older than you
And you’re one of Yevgeny’s precious scholarship girls.”

I do not stay in the doorway long enough
To ask myself

Or Remington whether
Señor's or Yevgeny's disapproval
Is worth a second's thought.

All I hear is precious.

The buttons on my shirt

Are easy to undo.
"Beautiful,"
He breathes.
But I know he has stolen this sight
Before—
Backstage on tour
In the poorly curtained dressing room.

He peels off his sweater,
Leads me to the couch,
Where the tie-dyed blanket
Turns out to have a dusty smell
Of its own.

His body presses me down
Into the unresisting cushion.
His hand slides
To that place on my neck
That makes me shiver.
His other wraps my naked waist.

Kisses take on a rhythm of their own,
Heads twisting side to side.

My back arches.
His lips are still too wet
But I love the feel of his skin against my skin.

My vibrating cell phone
A jolt of interruption
I cannot make myself ignore.

Could it be my mother calling with tragic news?

My father with a question about my bank card?

It is Julio,
His voice low.
"Dad is asking where you are.
I can't stall him forever."

"That was Julio.
I've got to get back.
I'll be in a ton of trouble."
I pull on my shirt,
The buttons suddenly a challenge.
Push my hair
Into something like order,
Pick up the motorcycle helmets

From the floor.
Rem sighs,
Tumbles himself off the couch.

I blink
At the sullen look that flashes
Across his eyes.

But it disappears
As he turns his sweater
Right side out,
Takes a helmet from my hand,
Moves toward the door.
"No more dancing for us, tonight."

I follow him again, unsure
About the rest of the steps to this dance
We are doing
Or maybe
If there should be
Any more.

The name of the little girl

Gifted with the Nutcracker doll
Varies from ballet company to ballet company,
Production to production.

Clara or Marie,
Alone onstage as the ballet begins,
Cherished and protected
By the dancers in the wings,
Beautiful in her ballet slippers,
Soft, white dress.

Lisette played her when she was nine,
Madison at ten,
Bonnie, too.

A rite of passage for the best girls
At the Jersey Ballet,
Who count their way
Through the grand costumes of the Christmas ballet
That marks the years
Better than birthdays.

"Oh, remember when we were Bonbons
Under Mother Ginger's skirt?"

"I had to be a boy in the party scene for three years!"

Bonbons
Party Children
Mice
Candy Canes

Twenty-odd December nights
Onstage
Eyes bright
Remembering why they dance.

Then on to Snowflakes
And beyond.
Dew Drops,
Chinese Tea.

Until finally, a chosen few grow up to dance
The longest solo, full of pirouettes and daring balances,
Escorted by the noblest partner—
The principal role in the ballet world's star production—
The Nutcracker's Sugar Plum Fairy.

In elegant pink tulle, elaborate tiara,

She mesmerizes the audience
And little Clara in her simple frock,
Who hopes, dreams of a candy-perfect world
Where nightmares turn to
Dreams come true.

December leaves little time

For stolen kisses.

At Upton, my adviser
Asks if I am getting enough sleep.
As if there were time between school, dance class,
Rehearsals, homework,
Bus rides, car trips.
Envying Julio and Simone,
Paul and Don, Katia and Barry.
Daydreaming about what might happen
Between Remington and me.

I just sigh, eyes down, say,
"*The Nutcracker* is a busy time.
But fun!"
Force a smile bright enough
To make him ignore
The nap I try to take
While our advisory group
Discusses Secret Santas
For the party I will miss
Because of the matinee that day.

The Nutcracker has stolen Christmas.

It is the villain Drosselmeyer
To my undanced Clara.

My parents are coming to see me dance on Christmas Eve.
I will sleep in their hotel room,
Trade presents under the Marriott tree,
Eat at a breakfast buffet
Dressed with fake mistletoe.

Then back to the theatre, the Snowflake unitard,
The tight silver cap.

Lisette has been given the chance
To dance the Dew Drop Fairy.
Madison and Bonnie
Take turns in the Chinese variation.

I am a baby,
Stuck with Simone and younger girls.
No beribboned tulle skirt
No lacquer red jacket and black eyeliner
No chance to be anything but first in an anonymous row
Of clinging, colorless
White.

I know rows and rows of people

Sit beyond the glaring lights of the *Nutcracker* stage,
Ooh and ahh at costumes, virtuosic steps,
The precision of straight lines.

But from the cavernous raft of the stage,
I see only an ocean of murky shadows before me.

The music moves the dancers together.
Hours of rehearsal breed a warm familiarity.
We each do our part.

In the wings, the soloists and principals
Stretch their calves, adjust their shoes.
The corps dancers scramble to dressing rooms
To change from one costume to another.

The younger dancers stand in awe—
Hope some magic
Will drip from the sweat of the real dancers' brows,
Some whispered secret
Will tumble from their lips.

It is all exhausting,

Occasionally exciting,
Sometimes strangely mundane.

Turning my mind
To memories of solos performed
Before a too-close row of folding chairs
In Ms. Alice's basement,
Where I could see every approving face
In a human-sized space.

I have never kept a New Year's resolution.

Never been good at studying for tests
Or brushing my teeth every morning before school.
Before I came to Jersey
My mother did my wash and folded it
In a neat pile at the end of my bed.

Julio watches me lug a damp armload
Of tights I could not wait to finish drying,
Dump them on my bed
While he stands in the doorway.

"Prospero Año Nuevo!"
He snorts at my confusion.
"Happy New Year."

"You too."
But it is no different
From any other day,
Except that this is the end of *The Nutcracker.*
There will be a party after the performance tonight
And Remington will be there.

I lead my line of Snowflakes

In a series of ports de bras, tendus, soutenu turns.
We run in delicate, toe-pointed circles,
Arms open in second,
Faces bright.

Finally pose
In low first arabesque,
Heads inclined
Toward the gracious Snow Queen and her consort.

One last time, we hold still
In two neat rows of eight,
As paper snow wafts down
Onto our silver-capped heads
Gently as burnt ash
From the tips of a thousand cigarettes.

In the dressing room

Lisette says a tearful good-bye
To her beautiful Dew Drop dress,
Tearing one tiny flower
From the shoulder strap.
A memory that looks
Like it will break her heart.

I want nothing from my costume
Except to forget it.

Will he give me another chance?

I think I have disgusted him
With my childishness,
Even though I am more afraid
Of being lonely
Than of losing anything
Rem could take from me.

At the party he hangs out
With Paul and Don,
Vincent, Marie, and Galina,
Until our eyes meet
Over the top of his beer.

He glances around quickly.
Is he looking for Jane?
Some disapproving teacher?
An escape
From my desperate gaze?

But no,
He comes over to my side,
Gives me a sort of fatherly hug.

Though his wide hands grip my forearms,

It is my heart
That feels the tightening
Of his fists.

"Long month, huh?"

I nod. "No more white unitard!"

He grins. "I liked it."

"That gaudy horror? How could you?"

"Well . . ."

I feel him trace my body
With his eyes.
Panic
Numbs my fingertips.
Desire
Makes my face burn.

"Want to go somewhere else?"
I hear my voice say.

A short, cold motorcycle ride,
Up the dingy steps again,
Past the tie-dyed sofa,

To Rem's bedroom,
Where I start the new year
Changed.

Afterwards

There is not much pain
But a surprising amount
Of blood.

The second of January

Is a Sunday.

I stay in bed pretending
I have nothing to hide.

At lunchtime Julio knocks,
Pokes a deck of cards
Through my cracked-open door.

The giggle in my throat
Surprises both of us.
Can I be hungry for something other than Rem?

The kitchen smells of refried beans,
And strangely delicious.

We gorge ourselves on laughter,
Scoring thousands of Rummy 500 points
Across the gold vinyl tablecloth
That always feels a little sticky
Despite Señor Medrano's fastidious housekeeping.

The television shouts in Spanish,
Battling the ferocious hum of the teacher's vacuum cleaner.

Señora has left again today.

I suspect that Señor is waiting for a phone call, too.
Can you still feel
Abandoned
After years of marriage, a child, artistic acclaim?

"Rummy!"
Julio jumps up.
Cards scatter.
I laugh again.
I can't help myself,
Though it makes me ache.

At the studio on Monday,

I am early for class, as usual,
Thanks to Ruby Rappaport's lack of regard
For speed limits.

I stand alone at the barre,
Work my feet
Through a series of slow tendus,
Try not to look in the mirror
For the girl
I can't get back.

A shadow passes
Over my shoulder.
Rem's hand is on the barre behind me.
I feel the breath of his words
Against my back
So I know he's not looking
In the mirror
Either.

"I'm working on a new piece
After Variations tonight.
If you want to . . ."

I steal a peek
At his reflection
On the far wall.

Rem's voice is casual but
His spine has an electric straightness that makes me dare
Regard my own silhouette as I say,

"Yes."

Señor Medrano doesn't mind

My change of schedule
As long as I can get another ride home
So he can get back to the dusting, the supper,
The world outside the dance studio
Where he seems almost joyful
To relinquish his teacher crown.

Other dancers sometimes stay later, too:
Vincent and Fernando,
Simone,
Company dancers working on projects
Of their own
While Remington makes dances
Then flies me
On the back of his motorcycle,
Pulls me
Up the three flights of stairs,
To the surreal world of the musty couch,
The orange chairs.

Señor doesn't wait up,
Doesn't comment
On the lateness of the hour
That Remington returns me.

Though often,
When I tiptoe up the stairs,
Light seeps through Julio's cracked-open door.

In the morning, Julio doesn't ask
With anything but his eyes.

Bess emails me a picture

Of her and Stephen
On a snowshoe date,
Grinning and rosy against powder-white drifts,
Bundles of coats, hats, boots.

"His brother drove the truck,"
She writes.
"We made out the whole way home."

Rem laughs
When I show him, asks,
"Could he even find her
Under all those clothes?"

I giggle.
Roll against him.
There was no rehearsal tonight,
Just a made-up excuse
So Señor would leave me late
At the studio.

I like real rehearsal nights better.
Rem's eyes turn luminous
When music and steps collide,

His grip velvet steel
When he leads dancers
Through his choreography.

And after, he is gentler,
Unwound.

When he doesn't make dances
He is silly, but less tender.
Mumbles more often questions
I don't want to hear or ask myself.
"What am I doing with you?"
I feel like a distraction
Between his sheets.

"Want some water?"
He sits up.
The blanket twists around me.

I shake my head, no,
Roll over,
Lift Bess's picture
From the nightstand.
Smile back at the frosty faces.

City water gurgles from the kitchen sink.
A glass smacks against the tabletop.

I straighten the brown quilt, the beige sheet.
Wonder what I'd be doing
If I'd stayed home, in an orchard
Softly buried in Vermont snow.

At Upton I am asked to talk

To my classmates
About being a dancer.
"An opportunity for leadership," says my adviser.
Though I think he just worries
I don't have any real friends.

I sit in the Upton library
Rifling through index cards
On which I have written meaningless words
About discipline
Technique
Dedication
Strength
Resolve

Fiction

Not as powerful as *Crime and Punishment*
Nor as funny as *Never Cry Wolf.*

Dare I tell them that since I came here to dance
I have been giving pieces of my body away
To ridiculous diets,

To repeated injuries,
To Remington?

And that maybe
I think
With each bit of my body

I lose a little piece of my soul.

Instead I write a story

About the *Sleeping Beauty* variation.

How you have to understand
That the littlest développé of your foot
Contains the enormity
Of the most giant pirouette.
How in the small step,
The plié,
The beginning,
Is the climax,
The end.

I read it out loud
To a sea of blank faces.
They are thinking
Perhaps
How my thin, white neck pokes
From my dark red blazer.

My fingers slide up,
Crawl over
Pronounced tendons.
My voice fades away.

From the back of the room
My English teacher, Professor O'Malley,
Clears his throat.

"A little louder, please, Sara."
He speaks in an Irish brogue,
Usually strong,
Though today his voice
Sounds nearly as strangled
As mine.

Still my name
Lilts off his tongue,
Draws my hand
Back down to the page.

I read on.

Despite how much I hate *The Nutcracker*,

January at the studio
Is all rambling melody
Without harmonic interruption—
Flat.

I am exhausted from December,
More exhausted from stolen hours
In Remington's bed,
Where I am the princess of everything,
Also the palace slave.

At school we are reading
Paradise Lost,
Which is mostly amazingly dull
Even though it is about Adam and Eve
And all that trouble.

I understand that I have bitten
The forbidden fruit.
Still I cannot quite see
What the paradise was
Before.

Was it only the hope
Of being the chosen girl
Of being the great ballerina
Of being special?

Is paradise only
Possibility?

I write this question down

For Professor O'Malley.
(Not the part about my own sin,
But about paradise
Only being the hope
Of something else.)

It's really just because
I cannot do the assignment—
Something about imagery
That leaves me cold.
Plus I haven't finished reading
Milton's endless poem
By the date
On the syllabus.

In the margin of my graded essay
Is a handwritten request
For me to come see him
During office hours,
Which means I'd miss my safe ride
With Ruby Rappaport,
So maybe another time.

Denardio's is a crowd tonight.

Paul, Don, Galina,
Fernando,

Even Jane,

Who sits by Paul
Nursing a glass of white wine,
A soft smile behind her eyes
That once in a while
Takes in Remington
Even though, beneath the table,
He holds my hand.

Despite my efforts
To avoid her gaze,
I nearly walk straight into her
As I come out of a ladies' room stall.

"Hey, Sara."
Jane's voice is steady, casual.

My mind scurries around corners
Of embarrassment, fear, guilt,
Then leaps to a self-righteous memory

Of Rem and Jane arguing on a Saturday morning—
To Remington assuring me that there's no more romance
Between them.

I should at least say hi,
But my voice is stuck.
All I can do is run my fingers,
Slimy with industrial pink soap,
Under the cold water.

"It's okay." She runs a comb
Through her unruly curls,
Considers her reflection,
Adds lipstick.

In the sanitary stink
Of the pizza-place bathroom
My heart forgets to beat.

"You know, though, maybe you should be more careful
About Rem than you are about your shins."
She snaps the lipstick tube shut,
Takes a compact from her purse,
Consults the mirror.

Without stopping to sort
The meaning of Jane's words,
Just grateful for the turn of her back
That releases my frozen feet,
I tiptoe out
Through the narrow corridor
Into the comforting blare
Of Denardio's
Where I can bury my thoughts

In the buzz, grease, heat,

The press of Remington's thigh
Against mine.

Remington's apartment is cold

But he says that I inspire him
When I lie naked
On his bed.

He is choreographing
A new dance,
Though I cannot see
Where my scant, white self
Is reflected in the driving leaps,
The syncopated footwork
Of his ballet.

He didn't ask me
If I was having fun
Amidst the pitchers and pizzas tonight
While he grinned and laughed
In his easy way
Around the table.

I call him Rem
Because everyone else does.
In my head
He is always Remington.

Large, expansive, smiling,
Fine-haired
Fatherly
Kind
Cruel.

Dancing Aurora's Variation,

The lovely princess steps of the *Sleeping Beauty*
Wake my mind from its stupor
Of confusion.

We are given rehearsal skirts
To get the feel of our legs
Peeking from below the frothy folds
Of tulle.

I love learning this dance.
My arabesques are growing stronger

But my arms are never quite right.
I twist my wrists too much,
Bend my elbows too little.
Sometimes I cannot time
The ethereal, swirling ports de bras
To match my legs' sixteen soft développés.
The music catches up to me
Or seems to lead.

Señor Medrano draws exasperated fingers
Through his already stand-up hair.

In the car
On the way back to his house
He clears his throat.
"Sara, you work hard, yes.
But on tour dis spring
Bonnie will dance Aurora.
She turn sharp! Yes?"

My mind paints Bonnie's picture.
She moves stiffly,
A skeleton clown,
Graceless yet precise.
Can this be better
Than what I do?
That jerky scarecrow
Always with the band of white elastic
Around her waist?

"Sure,"
I squawk.
Feel my face burn,
Glad I've taken down my bun
So perhaps Señor cannot see
The color of my cheeks,

Though I do not know whether they have turned
To red or white.

"Bonnie, she work hard, too.
Get arms very soft. Steps steady."
Señor grips the wheel tight
Like Dad.
Stares out at the dimming road.

I know the meaning of averted gazes.

On my dresser is a postcard

From Ms. Alice:
A Russian ballerina in black and white,
Arms open, reaching forward,
Leg behind in arabesque.

"Anna Pavlova."
Ms. Alice's handwriting loops in even curves.
"She reminds me of you.
Keep working hard!"

I sit on my narrow bed
In the dank room
Where only strains of Julio's guitar
And his occasional muttered curses
Filter through the door.

I think of Ms. Alice, Mom, Dad, eyes full of pride.
Bess, the practical genius, sending me off.

Wish there were no photographs,
No mirrors in the world to record
Anna Pavlova
Or Lisette or Bonnie or Rem,
But especially my own reflection.

"C'mon. Get up!"

Remington grabs his rumpled jeans from the floor,
Gives them a shake.
"We've got to get back to the studio."

"Five minutes," I mumble.
The lunch break during Saturday rehearsals
Is plenty of time
To steal away to Remington's
And be back in time for subtle, separate entrances
Through the studio door.

So no one will suspect
What everyone knows.

But I am tired.
The bed is warm.
I luxuriate in the lack of music,
The pile of blankets,
The soft shards of sunlight
Slanting through the venetian blinds.

He fumbles for his sneakers.
"C'mon!"

"Okay. Okay."
I draw my knees beneath me,
Arch my back upward,
Head still on the pillow,
Bun still half pinned in my hair,
Arms stretching up and to the sides.

"Sara!"
Rem squawks.

My head shoots up.
"What?!"

"Do that again."
He is whispering now.
"That stretch in the bed."

Barely remembering
But frightened by his tone,
I put my head back down,
Wriggle my knees underneath,
Try . . .

I feel his arm
Lightly

Over me.
He takes one of my outstretched hands.
Draws it beneath my stomach.

"One more time . . ."

This is not sex,
Not friendship.
Something
Strange
Special
In the stillness of his breath,
The waterlike way he moves.

He is making a dance.

We are making a dance.

I do not care about Aurora anymore

And her mincing variation.
Princesses are weak
Compared to the force
Of a muse.

Now
I intoxicate him.
My body a song,
Magnetic as the voices
Of the sirens from Greek mythology
I studied in eighth grade.

We dance behind his couch,
Around the orange chairs,
Over the bed. And after
The sex is something
That I did not know
Before.
He watches me sleep.
Waits for me to stretch, bend.

In the studio
I feel his eyes on my back,
Protective, searching.

I nestle in the clouds
Of his obsession,
Thick, enveloping round
My bright star.

Though sometimes
The density of his gaze
Chokes my lungs,
Weights my feet.

And, other times, I worry
I am giving away something
More precious
Than what Rem has already taken.

I try to write about the creation

Of a dance

In words I can safely say
To Professor O'Malley.

Try to describe
The pressure,
The lightness,
The relief when hands touch,
Legs extend,
Movement flows through music
Or without it.

Milton's *Paradise Lost*,
That ceaseless poem
Of beginnings and mistakes,
Takes shape in my mind
As two ballerinas
And I understand
Why the poet
Needed to write those words.

But my words feel weak.
Everything has shifted

From my pencil
To my feet
To Remington's eye.

So I am almost relieved
To hear about Rem's five-day intensive
For young choreographers
In New York City.

He tells me as I lie
Obligingly exposed
Across his narrow mattress
While he packs his things.

Still, it is hard to go to the studio

Without Rem there,
To watch Bonnie and Lisette
Rehearse their solos.

So at last I stop
At Professor O'Malley's door.

"You wanted to see me?"

"Sara, yes, one moment if you please."
Irish accent, as usual,
Turns my name to poetry.

He fumbles with the stacks of paper.
"Your essay on Milton."
His hands search the towering piles,
Fan through thick folders.

"I brought my copy."
I take it from my backpack,
Set it on a tiny, exposed corner
Of mahogany.

"Yes." A grin spreads.

He skims the pages.
"It is very good,
Like your essay about dancing.
You write well."

He lilts on
About connecting ideas
To events,
To images.
About capturing movement
With language.

I feel my weight release
Against the doorframe,
Consider the possibility
Of making myself
A nest of the stranded papers
In this cluttered room,
And never riding the ogre bus
To the studio today.

Yevgeny's eyes are black.

They watch not just the muscles
But the bones inside.
Dissecting every step.
Looking for flaws
For missed potential
For what might ultimately be unattainable
By this shape, this form,
This girl.

Today they smoke
In my direction.
I was late to the studio,
My bun unkempt.
I can feel my period coming,
My stomach a swollen mass
Of pressure and foreboding.

I forgot to eat lunch.

The studio turns starry.
I grab the bar,
Feel my leg plummet downward—
Grand battement
Defeated by gravity.

"Sara?"

Yevgeny's voice is sharp.

"I'm okay!"

I run to the dressing room,
Throw up in the nearest toilet stall.
Curl into a ball
On the cool, black-and-white tile.

I don't like being sick away from home.

I loll on the yellow couch,
Eyeing the plate of crackers,
The cup of tea
Left for me
On the black lacquer coffee table.
Wish for a down comforter,
Homemade toast with cinnamon sugar.

But I allow Señora to pass a wet cloth across my face,
To ply me with sweet tea,
To look concerned
As I watch the clock count hour after hour
That I lie still without dancing,
And talk on my cell
To my real mother.

Rem and I return on the same day

To the studio.

Four days in bed
And I am better.
Rested.
Fed.

Rem is on fire
With dancing, ideas.

I doubt that he would like me to tell him
About the tortured journey
Of *Paradise Lost*
As much as he likes
To ride the shallow slope
Of my naked behind.

Yevgeny shows no mercy

In Variations class.
It's as though I never left.

He looks up and down
At me, through me, trying to read
Something I have not printed in my face,
Because I do not know it,
Cannot give him an answer
To a question I don't even understand.

Only knowing I want always
To be the girl in front.

Instead I stand behind beaming Bonnie,

A faceless head
In the second row
Of the corps ballerinas,
Ladies-in-waiting
For her precise, twiglike Aurora.

Watching from behind
Sliding bobby pins,
Fingers furtively tugging

Down
Leotard leg holes,
Fixing, adjusting
What cannot be seen
On the facade
Where the smile is wide,
The hair slicked back,
Neck long, chin high,
Everything forward,
Yearning
Toward the teacher,
The mirror,
The hope that lives
Beyond the glass.

The back row
Stinks of despair,
Surreptitious farts,
The breath of disappointed curses.

Is truth here
In the ugly unseemliness?
The graceless moments
Before and after

Eyes are watching?
In the unballerina,
The unperformed?

In the dressing room
I forget to be embarrassed
As I write down this other question,
Sweating through my half-off leotard,
Smeared mascara soiling my cheek.

In my mind Professor O'Malley's brogue
Singsongs a perfect
Three-word refrain:

"You write well."

For a moment,
More beautiful than Tchaikovsky's music,
More powerful than being Rem's girl.

It must be serious

Because Mom has come.
She and Dad sit across from me
In a darkened booth
At Denardio's.

A snapshot
Of my first kiss with Rem
Here at this table
Sears my mind's eye.

I worry they can read past the heat of my cheeks
To the confession
That pumps my heart.

But the conversation's focus

is on my glorious PSAT scores
And the letter from Upton
That says I will be
A National Merit semifinalist.

This has led my mother,
Crisp in her navy-blue suit,
Lacy under-blouse,
A failed attempt at femininity
(She could use a lesson from Señora Medrano
And her tight silks),
To swoop down to Jersey
With a stack of brochures
From colleges I have never heard mentioned before.

"But I thought you wanted me to be a dancer."
The words escape my lips before
The thought reaches my brain.

I make up an excuse about a late rehearsal

To avoid sleeping in their sexless hotel room.
Sneak away to Remington's,
Where I am still a ballerina.

He sits on the tie-dyed couch,
Eyes closed,
Bach cantata playing over and over.
Tries to find the steps
That will meet the music.

I wait,
Ineffectually reading
Professor O'Malley's next reading assignment,
Saint Joan by George Bernard Shaw.
Though saints and martyrdom
Do not feel at all connected
To my confused existence.

I know that, sooner or later,
Rem will tire of his tortured artist solo,
Remember the magic of his muse,
His dick,
The bed.
Blush to think of my parents

Imagining me here.
Ponder whether Señor Medrano, Yevgeny
Know,
Even suspect
What Remington does with me
After the studio is dark and
The other ballerinas have gone home.

Am I the great actress of innocence,
The pure Aurora, despite Bonnie's better musicality?
Is it worth their averted gazes
For the dances that Rem makes?

Should I shout (as if I ever could),
"This is wrong!"
Is it wrong?

Sometimes you can smooth a fumbled balance
Into another step;
Cover a weak arabesque
With a flourishing port de bras;
Keep your smile so bright, head so high,
They overlook the weakness of your feet.

Feints of the body not unlike
A magician's sleight of hand.

When he introduced *Saint Joan*, the author
Told readers there were no villains in his play—
That crime was not nearly so interesting
As what men and women do
With good intentions, or believe they have to do
In spite of what they feel.

"Hey, thoughtful."
Rem slides a playful hand across my stomach.
"Ready to dance?"

"Stop

Letting your stage parents
Push you around," Rem says
After I describe our conversation.
He yawns and stretches,
Circling the white stem of my waist
With a possessive arm.

"They are not stage parents,"
I snap.
But I am glad he doesn't like them,
Enjoy the battle
Between king-and-queen
And knight in Lycra armor.

They want to take me
To an orthopedic surgeon
To help resolve
The pain in my shins.

Rem says they are looking for a way
To stop me from dancing
Now that they have decided
I am a genius.

I do not believe him
Until later, over coffee,

Mom suggests
We take a trip to visit colleges
And that I can easily miss
A week of ballet class.

Her eyes flutter to some invisible thing
In the corner of the room.
Her fingers roll the brown, raw sugar packet
Into a determined cylinder.

Dad watches her hands—
The brown roll cigarette-like,
Tempting—
Eyes down.

I won't go

Even though the chance
To run away from all this mess
Holds a certain appeal
And I am just a little curious
About these universities
Katia and Anne
Discuss with bright eyes,
Damp with anticipation,
As if they see that paradise
Milton claims we all have
Lost.

After two days of trying

Mom throws up her hands,
Mutters about a business trip.

Dad escorts her away
Right after an early breakfast.

I watch him drive,
His eyes fixed on the road
So I will not see the sadness
I know they hold.

I am like him:
Drive, drive, drive,
Afraid of the dark,
Even more terrified to stop
To think what it all means.

I am the proud owner
Of three new pairs of tights
To save me so much washing,
Two expensive leotards,
No more because Mom says
That soon there will be changes

(In her mind, college;
In mine, that I will move up a level).

Buying too much
Hunter green
Will be a waste.

I hold a giant file of college brochures
That I have told them will also be a waste.
But I took them anyway.

I don't know why the cheap novels bother me,

Since waiting is a giant feature of ballet.
Waiting for your ride—
Your class—
Your rehearsal—
Your turn.

Yet somehow I begrudge
The beautiful professional ballerinas
Their stupid, time-killing romance novels.
It seems to me
There must be something more.

Would it be strange to offer
A Tale of Two Cities,
The Moon and Sixpence,
Ragtime?

They think I'm weird enough already.

Professor O'Malley's office is neater

This time.
Swathes of mahogany in view
Between the sheaves of paper.
A silver cup filled with pencils
Red and blue.
A delicious, musty smell
Like Ireland in my imagination.
The place where George Bernard Shaw was born;
Wrote so many words
About poor and rich, people
And saints,
Plays, novels, criticism.
Refused recognition,
Knighthood,
Even the money that came with a Nobel Prize.
Died from injuries gotten from falling
While pruning an apple tree.

This time,
Professor O'Malley speaks of the story
I wrote about *The Nutcracker*
And the little children peering from under the skirts
Of Mother Ginger.
Tiny lost souls

Who do not yet understand
That they are on a stage,
That beyond the footlights
People are watching;
Who only dance
Because their bodies are so light,
Because the music carries them.
The lilting melody
To which they dance
Is a Pied Piper's song.
And, like the children of Hamelin,
They do not know
That they are prisoners.

It is strange to hear my words
Read back to me.

I don't think I wrote them
To have them ever leave the page.

I think I only write
What happens across my brain
When my feet are too weary
To dance anymore.

Professor O'Malley
Says that it is more than that,
That I have something to say.

I shake my head to disagree.
My hair, not in a bun yet,
Shoots down my back, clean and slick.
My maroon blazer lolls over my arm.
A ruffled, white shirt, another legacy of Mom's visit,
Gives me a certain shape.

"No. No, Sara,
Do not diminish yourself like that."
He puts his fine, girl-like hand on my shoulder.

I feel something
In the air
That makes me think of Remington.

His dance is finished

So he sleeps.
"Not now, Sara."
Remington's response to my wriggles
Beside him.

He tells me I don't understand the pressure
Of choreography competitions,
Artist-in-residence applications,
Fighting for opportunities to shape his dances
Onto ballerinas.

The words "explain it to me"
Catch in my throat.
I have heard him tell Paul and Don, Jane,
About his worries.

If he fails,
Will he blame
His muse?

Now Julio is packing

For a student retreat
With his music school.

"Think Simone will miss me?"
He winks.

But Simone is full
And ripe with gossip, friends,
Unafraid to tease and crush,
To ask for things she wants

More than what the teachers,
The mirror, tell her.

In the bathroom at Señor Medrano's

Julio's electric razor
Sits forgotten on a shelf over the sink.
Sometimes when we play cards,
I search his face for the need
For that razor.
See only a fine, soft stubble
Over his lip—
No hairs to create
Evening shadows on his chin, his neck,
Like Remington's.

When we laugh together,
Perhaps I should flirt with Julio,
Playful,
Like Remington still flirts
With Jane.

Is it fair to like apples *and* peaches,
Steps *and* letters,
More than one boy . . .
Are you allowed to love like that?

Alone in the house with Señor Medrano.

Dinner is a torturous affair but
For some inexplicable reason
I don't want to go to bed
With Remington.

Give my Saturday to dancing.
Half the night, reread
Professor O'Malley's scrawls
Commending my language, imagery, ideas,
My ear for the lyrical movement of words,
Something Yevgeny has flatly said
My dancing lacks.

Sunday, exhausted, nap,
Fan the pages of teen magazines,
Where I read about unwanted pregnancies, STDs,
The kinds of protection Rem taught me to use.

These things are less real
Than my loneliness
When I slide out from beneath Rem's sheets,
Watch him chatting on the phone
With Jane, who has agreed
To be "just friends."

Sex is a price to be paid
For company.
For a second I consider whether Professor O'Malley
Would trade it for kind words
About my worth.

Shannon watches me limp

Out of her class
On Monday afternoon.

"Come here, Sara.
Let's have Jane take a look at those shins."

Unable to refuse a teacher,
I follow Shannon
To the physical therapy room,
Listen to her talk about me
With Jane.

"I'll leave you to it, then."
Shannon waves her graceful, silver-ringed hand.

"I've got to head out in a few minutes,"
Jane says to me.
Her voice is measured, professional.
"Let me see when I can get you on the schedule."

"Okay."
I hover near the safety
Of her office door,
Nod as Simone, Bonnie, some others pass by,
Watch jealously as they settle onto the hall benches,

Tuck away their pointe shoes, chatter about their day.

"Have a good weekend, Sara?"
Jane does not look up from her computer.

"Uh-huh."

"What'd you do?"
Still steady, now, but Jane's voice
Rises in pitch.

"I . . . um . . ."

"You disappear all weekend.
He doesn't make any dances.
Now you're back and he's left to imagine
Who it is you sneak off to be with.
You torture him."

My eyes swell open,
Seized by dampness.
I am not breathing,
Just standing there
Pulsing
Red.

In all those words
She doesn't say his name; still

Out in the hallway,
The wide circles of the other girls' eyes
Show she was not quiet
Enough.

"I can see you Wednesday at two,"
Jane finishes, her tone sweet
As if the words that came before
Were as innocent.

I know I won't keep the appointment
Even as I nod acquiescence, limp back down the hall
Without stopping at the crowded benches.

Later,
In my narrow bed
At Señor Medrano's house,
I think of my reply.

"But *Rem* is torturing *me*."

My cell phone buzzes.

I jump from my bed.
It is not Remington,
Just another text from Bess.
Going to a jazz concert
With Tina and Kari,
Saying she is sick of boys.

I giggle at Bess's dramatic statement
Until my eyes fill with missing
A friend who knows how to tap a maple tree,
And help her dad mend a stone fence.

What would Bess have said to Jane?

How can Jane know
These things about me and Remington?
Can there be a friendship
Between Rem and Jane
Like there is between Bess and me?
Or has that friendship, too, become surreal,
Shattered
By my secrets and omissions?

Afraid to make another enemy,

I text back a vapid
"Cool. Have fun."

Despite the late hour, a soulful Latin melody
Rises through the hall.

I lie still.
Let the guitar strings pulse
Through the twanging nerves of my body,
Stare at the bare, white walls, missing the slick posters
That smiled out at Bess and me
So many innocent nights
While speakers blared big-band music
To fill us up,
Shut out the ordinary.

Can I pretend to be sick?

I am terrified to go back to the studio.
Terrified of Jane,

Of who or what I am—

A pulsing mass of bone
And muscle,
Burning face, feelings
I am afraid to try to sort or organize
Or understand.

I feel naked
Even as I pull on my khaki pants,
White shirt.

So long invisible:
Mama Bear, not Goldilocks,
Outside the social circles of Upton.

Overnight
I will be the subject of every dressing-room conversation.
The villain of Jane's story.
A bad girl.

Me with the pocket full of vitamins
Who always buckles her seat belt.

Now I will be glad to pose behind
Bonnie's taut Aurora.
Keep my hand down in English class.

Today is much worse
Than the morning after my first night
With Remington.

I stuff clean tights
Into the purple ballet bag,
Zip the backpack closed,
Walk out to the school bus stop
Without any breakfast.

I make the mistake

Of walking past the headmaster's door,
Cracked open as usual,
The murmur of intellectual conversation
Buzzing into the hall.

"Sara?"
The high, cerebral voice
In an unpleasant key.

"Um, yes?"

"Where is your blazer?"

In my morning haste
I left my burgundy jacket
On the knob of my bedroom door.

"That's a detention, you know."

From the doorway, I see him write my name
On an evil piece of paper.

"But I have to go to dance class!"

He will hear no excuses,
His expression accuses.

I want to call my mother,
Turn her persistent, self-righteous energy
Toward the injustice of my dress-code demerit.
Have her restore
My unblemished record.
Remake me the picture of innocence.

A cell phone call during school hours
Is another infraction.
Do I dare?

There is no way, after all,
To set her on Jane.

I find Ruby Rappaport downstairs

Outside the senior lounge.
Tell her that I will not need a ride.

She grins at my story.
Pats me on the back.
Beckons.
"I have an extra blazer in my locker.
Just go back and show Headmaster Smith
That you put one on."

That afternoon
The windy fever of her topless car
Is intoxicating.

Simone draws me into a corner

As soon as I arrive at the studio.
"You should have slapped her."

I think of Julio
Drawn to her buoyant certainty.

Bonnie offers
One of her wide, warm smiles.

The knot in my stomach
Uncoils
Enough to dance.

Remington is at the far end of the barre.

We rarely speak in class,
Though we never discuss the reasons
Señor would disapprove.

I worry what Rem knows,
Whether he's spoken to Jane
Or heard the tale from one of the thousand girls
Who were in the hallway last night.

I watch him do six slow tendus,
Grab the barre,
Lean away to stretch his rippling arms,
Head back,
Breathing deep,
Lips set together, curving faintly upward.

If he is ignorant,
He is the only one.
I feel veiled glances
From all directions,
Simone's and Bonnie's comforting touches
On my shoulder.

I sink into a split.
A lazy act.
Splits are easy for me.
My hips relax too far in such directions.
Bow my head over my right front knee,
Grab the arch of my foot with my hands.
Don't want to look up.

Señor's black shoes
Slide in front of me.
I hold my breath,
Count the seconds as he passes.
Try to tell if he hesitates longer
Before me
Than all the others.

Turn my head subtly
To look again at Remington,
Now swinging his legs
In loose grand battements
As if he didn't have a care,
As if he didn't feel even a little bad
For not calling me last night.

Upton is buzzing with semester grades

But I could not bring myself
To open the envelope
Sitting on the Medrano's kitchen table this morning.
Could not face more judgment.

Told Katia and Anne it had not yet come in the mail.

The slim packet weighs down my backpack
All the way to the studio dressing room,
Where I tell myself I am a ballerina
And silly school grades don't matter to me.

"You look worried,"
Bonnie whispers.
Her face is gray,
Fine beads of sweat above her mouth.

"Are you okay?" I ask.

Bonnie draws the back of her hand
Across her damp lips.
Nervous brows furrow
Above her stage smile.
"Maybe we're both a little off."

I smile back,
Mine a little more real.
I care less about my grades
Than she about the thickness of her waist.

"Let's go,"

I say as I head for the dressing-room door.
Bonnie follows.
Chatter and piano music make the hall air fresher.

I lead the way to the far end of the hall
Where the ballerinas sit,
And Remington.

"Hey, there."
He gives the faintest smile
As I drop on the bench beside him.

Maybe Bonnie makes me bold,
Sitting on my other side.
We slip into pointe shoes,
Draw the satin ribbons across our ankles,
Tie the knots,
Tuck them out of sight.

I feel Rem's thigh against mine,
Warm. Press back.
Lean my head a little onto
His arm, white with straight, brown hairs.
He smells a little of smoke,
A lot of coffee.

Bonnie stands.
Puts her back to the wall.
Snakes one leg up toward the ceiling:
A vertical split.

I tell myself Jane made it up.
I don't torment him
The way she said I do.

Rem plants a fast kiss
On the top of my head,
Then jumps away
As if I could sting him—
So fast I can't understand whether or not I am forgiven
Or need to be forgiven.

I slide my satin-cased feet
Beneath the bench,
Draw the report card from my bag,
Trace its sharp edge with my fingertip.

"Maybe you should open it."
Bonnie is red-faced from stretching upside down.
"Out is always better than in."

The envelope can wait

Until after ballet.

Bonnie and I
Find places at the center barre.

Remington likes the barre on the far wall,
The spot nearest the mirror.
He can only see his reflection
When he is working the left side.

I do not feel jealous that Remington
Gets to make his own dances.
I am a part of them,
Of their creation.

I have watched him sweat and roar
Play and replay
Bits of music

Move and bend
In the narrow space
Behind the orange chairs
In his apartment.

Watched him come and go.

His giant presence
Warm,
His absence
A still, moist air,
A hollow space
In my gut.

I do not tell him
I write about his dances.
I do not tell him
I write.

Would he be jealous that I can make things, too?

I do not tell him
Writing about dancing
Is becoming the only thing
That makes dancing
Make sense.

In center, the piano plays

A steady, adagio melody to accompany
Développé promenade.

Yevgeny sets the combination
A little bit differently
Each time.

Begin in first position, arms in fifth.
Or begin in the stage left corner,
Left foot front, right in coupé behind.

But always after a series of tendus, perhaps a pas de bourrée,
A high développé a la seconde,
Rond de jambe to first arabesque.
Then slowly, slowly promenade the standing leg
Around in one complete circle,
Keeping the arabesque high.

As you turn
The supporting foot clenches,
The thigh in arabesque grows heavier,
You reach your pointed toe to the ceiling,
Pull in your gut, your chin haughty,

Unwilling to admit defeat
By the laws of gravity.

Ballerinas are better than that,
Even though the accompanist's fingers
Seem to slow to a near stop.
Each note stretches.
Eight counts will never come.

The weight of grades, Remington's awkward kiss,
Make tonight an eternal promenade,
Everything pulling down.

After technique class

We break up for separate rehearsals.
Yevgeny takes Remington,
Lisette, and Fernando
To the small studio.

I practice the Little Swans,
A dance for a trio of girls,
With Señor Medrano.
Arms locked together with Simone and Madison,
Heads precise, feet sharp.

The music hums and builds.
We point, piqué, step,
Counting hard to stay together.
Win Señor's smile
Which makes the evening
Suddenly spin faster.

I am half grinning when I leave the studio.
Simone and Madison head for the dressing room.
"You coming?"

"In a minute."

At the end of the hall
Is the small rehearsal studio.
I peek inside,
Hope to catch a friendly glance,
A be-right-out gesture
From Remington.

Strains of a slow waltz
Carry through the cracked-open door.

In the mirror, I see the reflection
Of Lisette
On her knees,
Forehead to the floor,
Arms stretching back.
Rem is showing Fernando
How to reach for her hand
Pull it beneath her
Raise her from the bed—
Our bed.

I know this movement.
I made it with Rem
A Saturday not long ago.

Something catches in my throat
As Remington grins at me
Through the mirror
Points to the imaginary watch on his wrist
Motions me to wait.

And I can't help myself.

Remington turns up his stereo, grimaces,

Fine, brown mane
Tripping over his forehead,
Brushing his upturned nose,
Arms outstretched.

"What are you doing?"
I sit up on the couch,
Wrapped in his plaid shirt
That smells of ships and vinegar.

"I'm looking for a beginning
For my dance.
It isn't quite right yet."
His eyes are exasperated,
Though I know, for this moment,
Not at me.

"First position," I blurt.

Rem's expression shifts,
Exasperation
Now more directed.

"No!" I almost shout against
His don't-interrupt-me-with-childishness eyes.
Desperate to have him see my worth as mind, not matter,
Muse, not obstacle.
"When you first learn to dance.
When you are little,
Four years old."
I stumble for meaning.
Words cluster in my head:
Beginnings, births,
Sunrises, starts.
"First position."
I stand up. Toes pointed outward.

"I started ballet later. I was nine.
Before that, I did theatre," Rem says.

The length of his sentence takes my breath away.
Our relationship built more on movement
Than conversation. I do not know the story
Of how he learned ballet.
Nor does he know mine,

Though I can hardly separate ballet
From all my beginnings—
First memories, first performances.
"Sometimes I feel I've just begun to dance,
Since coming here.
I still don't know why they dared try me.
I'm really too old
To begin," I confess.

Rem grins,
Exasperation fading from his eyes.
Takes ten steps across the floor,
Uncrosses my arms,
Spreads apart the plackets of his
Worn shirt.
Studies the front of me.

"No, not too old."
Lifts me up,
Guides me back to his bed,

Beginnings forgotten.

Back at the Medranos

I put the college brochures under my bed
After I brush my teeth.
Pull the hairnet off my bun with care,
Tuck the bobby pins into their white box.

I vow to be more like Lisette,
To warm up longer in the studio
Before the teacher comes in,
Work through my arches,
Perfect my ports de bras
Instead of just dropping into easy splits.

Take more time afterwards,
Repeat any step
At which I failed during class.

Look for approving glances
From Yevgeny or Señor,

Whose touches are not electric,
Who want me only to be
A ballerina.

I wake up facedown

In my math notebook,
Damp from drool
That smudges the penciled equations
Solving for the area under the curve.
Most of my notations are incomplete;
Curves are mystifying from any angle.

Slide out of bed
Curtsy to my mirror
Raise my left leg back in arabesque
Promenade slowly
Holding my leg
Up.

Lisette, Lisette, Lisette,
Who dances my dance
Better than I ever could.

Grab my backpack and
The sealed, white envelope from Upton Academy
For the academic conference today.

My report card is half good:

The English grade is excellent
History okay
Math kind of tragic.

Dad's tone of sorrowful disappointment,
The angry threat of tutors from Mom,
Echo through the unpleasant telephone call
With my confused Upton adviser,
Who points out that my PSAT scores show clearly
That I can do better.

At the ballet school,
Despite my new push toward perfection,
My ears hear much the same,
Though I try to make my brain ignore it
Like I ignore Jane's flaming glances.

Rem calls me on the cell.
"Be at the studio later."

"Okay."

I do not ask him
Where he is

Nor why
He gave my steps
To Lisette.

He offers no words of comfort,
Just some standard missing-you stuff
I allow myself to believe little more
Than my adviser's unsurprising counsel,
Than Yevgeny's incisive critique
That my technique is improving
But my performance seems halfhearted.

It seems I am living
Believing
Doing
Most everything
In halves.

In English, we are on to *Heartbreak House*,

A play title that resonates through the hollow
Of my bones,
Though I put it aside to reread *The Thorn Birds*.
Despite my anger, fantasize
About Rem's massive body
Enveloping mine
In a shroud of delirious protection.

Professor O'Malley assigns
An essay on the notion of reality
In Shaw's great play.
He looks at me
Quite directly
As he gives the due date.

What is reality

Anymore?

I whisper my own name
As I get dressed for school.

I speak so little all the time.
My words mostly touch paper
Or spill out through my arms and legs and fingertips.
My voice feels raspy,
An unflexed muscle.

Señor Medrano makes my name exotic.
Professor O'Malley turns it beautiful.
Perhaps I should invent a step, a sign,
Since when I say it, it sounds like an echo.

A half memory
Of a summer's day.
When I was a number
That caught Yevgeny's eye.

Am I a number still?
Attached to a body,
Finite technique.

I barely speak to Remington,
Yet in his bedroom we make dances
He can give away.

Does it matter that people and things
Have words,
Have names?

If not,
Why read any book?
A litany of useless letters
Detached from bone, muscle.

Or are words the only things
That make the muscle, bone, memory, movement,
Person
Real?

“Sara!”

Señora Medrano’s husky alto calls my name
As if she knew
I needed to hear it
To be.

“Dinner! It ees getting cold.”

Señora Medrano is such a terrible cook
I almost crave the meat-laced peanut butter sandwiches
I have thrown away most weekdays since last August.

At the table, Julio,
Returned from his music retreat,
Scowls at the dry steak,
Pokes the burned tortilla with his fork.
Sneaks me a grin.
Watches as I try to be invisible,
A quality with value at this dinner table.

Señora asks Julio about his guitar practice.

“I’ve been playing nonstop for a week.
Thought I’d take the evening off.”

That raises Señora's eyebrows.

A weak giggle escapes my throat.
Julio adds his musical, deep chuckle.
Suddenly Señor is laughing, too.

"That steak is very bad," Señora admits.

"Uh-huh!"
Julio pushes his plate away.

"Dancers should never cook."
Her eyes flash at Señor.
"Teachers can cook."

Four laughs vibrate in harmony,
Warm
Delicious
Real.

A new semester

Has begun at Upton.
Anne sits in the middle
Of the brown couch in the student lounge,
Wearing a new burgundy blazer,
With shimmering dark-red fringe around the collar,
A sharp, narrow cut.

Katia and I are on either side,
Wearing the same things we wore before,
Waiting for the school day to begin.

I try to listen to the gossip
About Ruby and Adnan,
About the plans for the spring dance,
About the biology teacher who is divorcing his wife.

But my shins ache,
I have a giant blister on my pinkie toe:
Rewards for working harder.

We're back to tour rehearsals tonight.

I am still Mama Bear

For the spring tour.
And Rem is still my Papa Bear.

We fall back into our bumbling pas de deux
As easily as I fall back
Into his bed,
Though afterwards I often lie awake,
Memorize the curves and intersections
Of the cracks in the ceiling.
Search futilely for some pattern, some word,
Some way to understand

Why he gives the dances he makes on me
Away to Lisette—
Why this is all right—

While I wait for him to take me back
To my other, ugly bed
In Señor Medrano's house,
Which has begun to grow
A bit more attractive.

Are habits as hard to break
As routines are to begin?

This is the question I write
In my essay about reality
For Professor O'Malley.

(Not the story of falling back into bed with Rem,
But of my oft-failed promises to get to class early,
Stay at the studio late,
Work, like Lisette, on every weak movement,
Imperfect step.)

Is the sound of the war bombs,
Like the ones echoing in the distance beyond
Heartbreak House,
Just easier to get used to
Than to recognize?

Is self-delusion turned-out feet?
A way we're accustomed to stand?
Identity simply the place in the line
To which we've been assigned
By some tradition, some chance,
Someone?

Perhaps the trick about reality
Is as much rejecting the old place,

The old step,
The old bed,
As seeing in the mirror
Something different.

Katia and Anne are practicing
For the Upton talent show.
I try not to laugh as I watch
Their scuffling tap dance,
Imprecise arms.

"You should dance that Aurora thing
You always talk about,"
They tease.

I let them believe
I perform the great variation.
Did not tell them I was replaced
By dark-browed Bonnie,
That what I know best
Are the steps of the thickly padded bear
Distraught by hot porridge
And unmade beds.

I am afraid to dance at school
Even though these girls
Offer no more threat to me in ballet
Than I to them in college applications.

"The stage floor is too hard,

I might get hurt.

My teachers would be furious,"
I demur as I turn my feet out extra far,
Extend my neck,
Toss my hair like a prima ballerina.

I am pretty sure the myth of me
Is better than the reality.

My body is angry

After ballet class tonight.

I walk gingerly down the hall.
Barefoot.
Blistered.

Wash my face.
Brush my teeth.
Limp back to my room,
Shins stinging.

The ceiling at Señor Medrano's
Is pebbly but clean.
No cracks scurry from the corners
To distract my mind.

At home, in Vermont,
Mom painted my ceiling a soothing light blue
With pale yellow walls.
Covered my bed
With a plaid coverlet in baby-soft hues.
All very tasteful
In her style.

I pull Señora Medrano's bright, nylon quilt
Up to my chin,
Stare at the ceiling's white pimples,
Wonder which bed
I should sleep in.

Which bedroom I want.

What dream I should dream
If I could sleep.

The stack of college brochures under my bed
Slips a little. In the slim shaft of morning sunlight
Sliding in beneath the blinds,
The stone archways
Of the Stanford University quad
Wink like supermodels from one glossy cover.

I put down Upton Sinclair's
The Jungle:
The ravaging tale
Of slaughterhouses in Chicago
In the early 1900s,
Of hearty immigrant Jurgis Rudkus,
Whose work ethic yields him nothing
But grief.

My fingers stray to the slim propaganda
Of Stanford.
Smiling young people with rounded cheeks
Grin from every page.
Clean, bright buildings,
Captions like ECONOMICS, PHILOSOPHY, SCIENCE.

I try to imagine walking along sunny corridors

In ordinary shoes,

Shins not stinging, and no one
Asking me to bend or stretch,
To point my talent
Through my toes.

After a while
I put Stanford
Down beside *The Jungle*.
Pull a pair of tights from the closet floor.

Reject Rudkus's struggle,
College's bright utopia,
For a dark green leotard,
A velvet ribbon in my hair.

I practice piqué turns

Beside Madison and Simone
To the right
And the bitter left—
My clumsy side
Where everything is harder.

When I was younger,
In Vermont,
Ballet was the right.
I floated above the others,
A little proud.
Easy
To dream
When you've turned
The right way.

Here, trying to be a ballerina
Often feels like a step to the left.

Señor Medrano comes into the studio.
His character shoes squeak. He announces

We have learned the Little Swans variation
Well enough to perform it on the tour.

We will be sewn into tutus,
Old but lacy.

Some newer girls
Eye us with jealousy
As Señor snaps commands;
We snap our heads
Right, left, right.

Jane smiles

When she passes me in the hall.
Her teeth are too white.
Her eyes too vague.

Can the scolding she gave me
Have faded in her memory?
The bright scar
Emblazoned on my brain
That makes me calculate the difference in our ages.

She does not mention
My missed appointment.
Carries a clipboard under her arm.
Heads purposefully toward her office.
Jane is staff
While I am a real dancer,
But her breasts stretch the front of her shirt
In a way that turns the straight boys' heads.

My head turns, too.
I cannot take my eyes from that Cheshire Cat grin,
So mesmerizing
I miss my footing,
Slam against the dressing-room doorway.

Smiles mean a lot of things:
Congratulations,
Forgiveness,
Victory.

Jane's sends a shiver down my spine.

At the Medranos' there is a long letter

From Mom,
Which is weird
Because she is a chronic, addicted texter.
Makes me wonder how busy she can be all day
At the bank.

When I lived in Vermont
Dad always came home first,
Dirty from hours in the orchard.
Dad started dinner.
Drove me to ballet class.

When I got back, Mom was always there
To check my homework,
Wash my tights,
Ask about my day.

Now I unfold
Three long, computer-printed pages
Of single-spaced
Times New Roman twelve-point.
Pages littered with words she rarely speaks:
How much she loves me.

How she worries about my future.
How she had such hopes for dancing.
How she wonders, now, if she guided me in the wrong
  direction.

After a while I can't read anymore.
Set down page two.
Tie on my pointe shoes.
Dance the Little Swans
Without Simone and Madison
In front of the narrow bedroom mirror.

My feet wobble on the shaggy rug.
My nose tickles with the scent of dampness,
Once revolting,
Now almost as comforting
As the smell of stale cigarettes
Lingering in the dark gray velour
Of Dad's well-kept Volvo.

I love the Little Swans,

The best dance I've been given
Since I came to Jersey,
Even though it's with two other girls.

The three of us drill and drill.

Señor Medrano smiles like he's just finished
Eating chocolates.
Pats our heads.
Sends us to wardrobe
To be fitted for skirts
Ready for the next round
Of school-tour stops.

Since starting rehearsals for this dance,
My pointe shoes are wearing through faster.
I am too hungry to resist
Señora Medrano's terrifying, oil-fried eggs,
Too tired to cry myself to sleep
Thinking of Jane's grin.

At Upton, Anne and Katia

Want to fix up
Their innocent ballerina friend
With some friend of Barry's
Who goes to another prep school
Down the road.

Bess IMs me about
A zillion boys a week
And the glories of second base,

And I reply
As if I don't know
Anything about that.

A week creeps by

Without a single kiss.

Each time Remington passes
In the hall,
Each syllable of his name
Conjures a movie in my mind.

Lisette
Forehead down
Arching
Reaching her hand
For him.

By Thursday, I feel a sting of desperation.

It is not exactly desire.
I am lonely,
Want
The comfort of Rem's heat.

I want Rem to tell me he'll protect me
From Jane,
From failure,
From the nagging fear that I am making the wrong choices.
From the dance I saw him teaching to Lisette and Fernando.

I linger near the studio entrance,
Hoping to see Remington's long, sauntering shadow
Cross the foyer.
But when he comes
He is talking with Jane.

I look down, fast.
Hear him say, "Hang on."

He walks over to me.
"Hey, Sara.

Why don't you wait a minute?
Just got to finish something up here."

All I can do is nod.
His eyes twinkle.
He makes a "stay there" gesture with his hands.

My legs go numb.
I slide down to the floor,
Pull *The Jungle* from my bag,
Pretend to read.

How long am I supposed to wait?

Staring at the jumble of letters
That swim before me
On the page.

Listening to the garbled whispers, gentle laughs
That waft from the conspiratorial mouths
Of Remington and Jane.

I try to strike a pose
Neither paranoid nor angry,
Hurt nor vengeful,
Nor even just curious about their conversation,
Though I am all of those things.

Head down,
I peek from beneath lowered lids
At Jane's arched back,
Fingers pushing back her coarse curls,
Face a study in controlled casual.
Rem's hand, occasionally touching her arm
Just above the elbow.

I watch Bonnie and Simone,

In street shoes, stop before me.
They look at Rem and Jane.
Look at me.

"Wanna walk over to the Rite Aid with us?"
Bonnie asks. "Simone needs hairnets."

"Rem asked me to wait."
My cheeks feel hot.
I don't look up.

"Well." Simone's hand is on her hip.
"Doesn't he have some nerve?"
Her voice is a stage whisper.
She makes no attempt at looking away,
Shiny black eyes send darts
In Jane's direction.

I whisper,
"I've got a lot of reading to do."

"If you're sure."
Bonnie hesitates.

Simone rolls her eyes,

Tugs Bonnie's sleeve.

"Well, okay then. Bye."

The book slips from my hands.

I pick it up.

Cannot find my page.

Adagio means slow,

Music sonorous, wandering,
Movements melting, blending, stretching,
Connecting the notes
Without coming up for air.

This night is all adagio.
Each second an hour.
Each movement unnaturally extended,
Painfully unreal.

"Hey, Sara."
Lisette plunks down beside me.
"What's that book?"

Is there a spotlight over my head?

"*The Jungle.*"

"What's it about?"
She scrutinizes the orange-and-black woodcut
On the paperback cover,
Absently peels a Band-Aid
From her index finger.

"A horrible factory, and
An immigrant trying to make it
In America."
I give the rote answer of a diligent schoolgirl,
Still trying to overhear the conversation
Happening down the hall.

"Oh. Ever read *Nory Ryan's Song*?
That's about an Irish girl trying to get to America."

I want to scoff.
I read that in fourth grade.
But it was a good book
And I have immigrated
To an alien planet
Where Remington is flirting with Jane
And the beautiful Lisette is asking me about books,
Not dancing.

"I read it first years ago," Lisette continues,
"But it's still one of my favorites."

I flirt with the possibility

That Lisette could be a friend.
But I would have to forgive her
For taking my dance,
As if she or anyone here knows
They should be sorry.

"Oh, there's my mom."
Lisette waves to a tall woman near the door.
"See you later."

The hall is nearly empty now.
Just a few others besides
Me against the wall,
Rem and Jane by the small studio,
Heads a little too close
To make my legs
Strong enough to stand.

The clock's second hand ticks adagio-slow
Past the one, two, three, four
Past the five, six, seven, eight
Past . . .

It's been too long since Remington

Glanced my way.
I force myself up,
Trace Lisette's steps
To the exit.

At the Rite Aid a block from the studio

I do not see Bonnie or Simone,
Who must have left
Before I found my legs.

I buy a giant bag of Nestlé chocolate chips
And a can of peanuts.
Eat half of them before I cross the parking lot
Back to the studio
And a ride home from Señor.

Wish I had Bonnie's courage to throw up.

I slide into my narrow bed

Alone.
Unwashed.

Books, tights, bobby pins
Overgrown in my jungle
Of a room,
A mind.

My stomach
Bloated from an unfamiliar feast,
I languish
In the pain of overstuffed body,
Clouded heart.

I shut my eyes.
See Rem's mischievous smile,
Long lashes,
Brown eyes,
Sharing movements with Lisette,
Laughter with Jane.

I said I would wait.
Am I a fool for not waiting?
Should I have pulled his shirtsleeve,

Arched my back,
Made some demand?

Should I have told Barry
I'd go with him to the Fall Formal?
Not waited the long bus ride,
The time for him
To grab his own courage,
Take his own chance,
Ask Katia?

Should I have said to Señor,
"No!"
When he said Bonnie
Would dance Aurora?
Should I have told him
I could do it?

Should I have stayed in Jersey
The weekend before the audition?
Sweated in the studio?
Showed my passion,
My worth?

I replay my stupid,

Foolish
Nod.
Rem's giant hands
Pushing air,
Telling me to
Wait.

Why do hands
Pushing air
Push me?

Why do I always
Time things wrong?
Go when I should stay?
Stay instead of go?

I wake up lonely.

Want to be

Someone's

Prima
Ballerina
Muse
Girl.

"You okay, Sara?"

Ruby Rappaport tosses
Her highlighted curls
Across her doll-like face,
Eyes concerned.

"Oh, sure."

"Haven't forgotten your blazer anymore?"
She smiles.

I laugh
As if I care.
Try to raise
My eyes
To meet hers,
My lips
Into a grin,
My heart
From my shoes.

In the studio
The air smells the same,
The mirrors still smeared,
The pianos still tinkling

Come-hithers
To the dancers in the hall.

But I am more different
Than on New Year's Day
When I thought I could own
Ballerina
Through Remington's embrace.

My feet so leaden,
I cannot imagine
I could ever dance
The picture in my mind.
The skipping four-year-old butterfly
In a basement studio
Catching Ms. Alice's eye.

Still I pin up a bun,
Slide into hunter green,
Ballet slippers.

Crawl into the studio
As if there were no other doors
In the universe.

Remington stands at his spot

Facing the barre on the far wall.
Pulls away to stretch, his back
Turned to me.

I sit on the floor
Beneath the center barre
Between Simone and Madison,
Bouncing my turned-out knees
Hard enough to make bruises.

He pivots toward the mirror,
Walks in my direction.
I drop my head to my feet.

Despite Señor's clacking heels
In the studio doorway,
Rem crouches down,
Touches my chin.
"It's not what you think, Sara."

Which can't be true,
Because I have thought everything.
Every possibility,
Combination,
Outcome,

Ends in a stalemate
Without conclusion.
And it must be one of them.

"Okay."
I add a false nod
Like the one I gave to Ruby Rappaport.

"We'll talk after class."
As if his smile
Commands
Acquiescence.

I stand up slowly,
In the aftermath
Of Remington's words.
Knees weak.
Breath fast.
Furious

At Rem for thinking
This could all be so easy,
At Jane for her power,
At Lisette for her pirouettes,

At myself

For nodding again,
For decisions that are always off count,
For not knowing the question
I would want him to answer
If I ever had the courage to ask.

Yet the venom strengthens my legs.
The anger steels my back.
The frustration clears my head.

When we get to grand battement
My leg kicks higher
Than any boy
Or girl
In the studio.
Kicks away
The regret,
The sorrow,
The uncertainty,
Up
Up
Over the streaks, smears, speckled fingerprints
To the top of the mirror where the clean glass
Reflects a sliver of pure light.

“Good job, Sara.”

Yevgeny finds me in the hall
After class,
Retying my pointe shoes
Before Variations.

He rubs his palms together,
Eyes thoughtful.
“Señor Medrano and I agree
It’s time to promote you to E class.
Get yourself some gray leotards
This weekend.”

I want to celebrate with Remington.

I can't help myself.

I sail through Variations
Without even stopping to care
About staring at Bonnie's
Skeleton back.

Afterwards,
I walk down the hall,
Into the small studio
Where Lisette and Fernando
Practice one more lift
While Remington makes notes
In a tattered, coverless
Spiral notebook.

"That's it. Thanks,"
He says to his dancers.

I skip up to him,
Almost not caring
Who is watching us.

"I'm in E class!"

And I am folded into his giant hug,
Smell his salty sweat, his nicotine breath.
Feel his damp, white T-shirt
Against my cheek.

Dad calls to celebrate the late frost

Which makes the sap flow quick.
"There'll be plenty of maple syrup
This year."

"Great."

As always, the metronome
Beats.

I know he will not ask me
Any real questions.
Everything is in the silence
Of his pauses,
The twitch of his fingers
Because Mom will not let him
Smoke cigarettes when he uses the phone
In the house.

I remember one Sunday.
I was nine years old.
Mom and Dad had had another quiet fight
About his smoking.
Mom packed a bag,
Bundled us into the car.

Drove down to the bottom of the hill
Just past the orchard gates.
Pulled to the curb.
Set the car in park.

We sat there, engine humming,
Her eyes brimming wet,
Me, uncertainly patting her shoulder from the backseat.

Twenty minutes later
She turned the car around
To go home.

All these years, through
Her myriad threats,
Newspaper clippings about cancer and heart disease,
His halfhearted stabs at quitting,

I somehow always knew:
Though he might never stop,
She would never leave him.

Señor Medrano gives me a serious look

When I tell him I am going out
With some friends.
"I'll get a ride home."

"Sah-ra, you have rehearsal all day tomorrow
And schoolwork.
Your parents, dey worry
About your grades."

"My essay for Monday
Is almost finished already.
Plenty of time to touch it up
On Sunday."

He shrugs.

What can he do?

I am not his daughter.
I am no one's daughter here.

"I miss you so much," he says,

Pushing a stray hair
Away from my eyes.

My body shudders.

"I can't wait for us to be together again."
There is something calculated
Behind his words.

"Remington?"

"I've got to work with some dancers
Tonight. It'll be late."

I watch him walk away.
Don't linger to check for Jane because
I have to find Señor Medrano
To get a ride.

Señor Medrano doesn't ask

About my change of plans.
Still I am glad
My cell rings in the car
On the way home.

"I'm promoted to E class,"
I tell Mom.

"That's wonderful.
You should exchange those green leotards
For the next color."

"Sure."

"Unless." She comes up for a moment's air.
"Did you cut the tags off already?"

"I did. Sorry,"
I lie.
Despite the expense
Measured in apples and peaches,
Forsaken weekend drives home.
Don't want the long explanation
Of how to make an exchange,

Her suggestions for the cut
Of the leotards I should buy,
To listen any longer
To Mom's rushing anxiety.

"I'll send you some money."
Mom is still talking.
"Don't forget to do your homework."

Ruby Rappaport has forgiven Adnan

For whatever offense he committed.
Now we speed even faster
Down the avenues,
Her head always half turned
Toward his tanned smile.

I clutch the white leather seat,
Wait for a complete stop in the studio parking lot
Before I undo the buckle.

In the studio,
I try not to look too desperate
Casting around for Remington.
Wishing I were a magnet that could hold his gaze.

Yevgeny's eyes do not breathe fire

When Rem comes late to class.
He holds a curious place
Between student and teacher.
Perhaps that's why they overlook
His tardy ways.

We développé and rond de jambe
While he pliés at the end of the barre,
Works his feet through slow tendus.

We grand battement, soutenu turn
While he coupés and jetés.

Later, at rehearsal,
My angry Mama Bear still swoons
Beneath his guiding hand
Beckoning me out into the woods
While, had I stayed to fan the porridge,
Goldilocks might not have upended our house.

During the break, Simone whispers,
"Rem's dance got second place
At the Young Choreographers Workshop.

He wants Yevgeny to add it to the repertory
For the tour."

I am not certain whether this is good
Or bad
Or who told Simone,
Though I suppose she knows everything
Except how to resist
That second donut,
Slice of pie.
Still her black hair shimmers.
Perhaps from buttery treats or not caring so much
If her Lycra uniform
Hints at a little softness.

"Girls!"
Yevgeny clicks his tongue from the doorway.
Simone giggles.
Red-faced, I scurry
Back into the rehearsal room
Where Lisette is already practicing bourrées.

I watch Rem's face for a smile

When Madison, Simone, and I
Finish a near-perfect Little Swans.
But I find it hovering
On Yevgeny's lips.
"That's right, Sara."

Remington's back is stiff.
He is staring through the mirror
Into some island no one else can see.

He is standing in second position,

Barely aware
He is not alone.

I pack my bag,
Watching his slow plié,
His pressed-together lips.

Second position
Second base
Second place

Not destinations—
Transitions.

Not first, not best,
Not last.

En route.

Can Rem be satisfied
With second?

When first place looms,
A taut and elegant Lisette,

Reflecting back your own missed
Possibility.

When you flirt with the mirror,
You never stand in second.
Yet, there he is,
Feet splayed.

Still, the invitation comes

Before I put my pointe shoes away.
"Denardio's tonight?"
Rem's voice is casual.

My shins ache.
Mom's latest letter and *The Jungle*
Wait unfinished in my bedroom.

I lift my chin to decline.
My eye catches Jane
Deliberately writing notes on her clipboard,
Pretending she is not listening.

"Sounds good," I say
Without checking his expression,
Just in case.

He is anxious, pacing

Near the doorway
When I emerge from the dressing room
In my uniform khaki slacks, wine-colored blazer.
"I didn't know we'd be going out."

"You look like a schoolgirl," he scoffs.
But he slides his hand under my jacket,
Rests it on my backside,
Hands me a helmet.

Remington zooms the motorcycle past Denardio's.
"Wait! Where?"
I holler over the choking breeze.
His answer just a muffled roar passing my ears.

We pull up outside a tiny Chinese restaurant,
Its front window ablaze
With golden, pagoda-shaped Christmas lights.

Rem leads me inside
Past a monster tank full of crimson carp,
A sign for the restrooms,
To a table for two.

He drops his long form into the chair closest to the wall
Sets the helmets under the table
Takes the menus from the waiter's hand.
"Do you like dumplings?"

I can count on one hand the times
I have eaten in a Chinese restaurant.
I remember white rice and stir-fried steak with broccoli
Before I learned that rice was carbs,
That red meat was dangerous,
That soy sauce had too much sodium.
Before I learned to be afraid
Of food.

"I don't know."

"You're gonna love 'em."
He pulls a cigarette from his jacket,
Twitches it between his index finger
And the middle one,
Rat-a-tat.

"A Tsingtao for me and a water for the lady

And a plate of veggie dumplings to start."

I look at his face
Across the table.

Is he so relaxed, confident
Because we are so far
From the studio?

Is he trying to apologize for something?

How does he know I will love dumplings any more
Than he knows I cannot ask
Any of the questions
That flood my mind?

He tips his head to light up,
His mellow, brown eyes twinkle.

"We're celebrating second place
In the Young Choreographers Workshop."
He raises his beer.
"I've been invited to the Blue Mountain Dance Festival,
Choreographer-in-residence
Next summer."

The clink of my glass
Against his frosty bottle,
Rem's wordless answer
To my unspoken questions.

This celebration he is having with me
Not Lisette
Not Jane.

Has it changed,

This thing I have with Remington?

His dance-maker, his muse,
His naughty secret
Who bundles beneath his covers,
Always cold
While he sleeps?

As I count the seconds before I wake him
To take me back to the Medranos',
I cannot fit our celebration
Into that equation
Any more than I can derive formulas
For calculating the area under a curve.

My math professor patiently tutors me, but
Remington
Does not.

Is there a formula in his mind?
Does he wonder at what we're doing?
Second-guess his inconsistencies?
Worry at my hesitations?

I begin to think the riddle
Is only in my mind.
In his, there is no need beyond
The flow of days,
Like the music he uses
To make dances.

The next night, I sit beside Barry

At the Upton talent show.
He never speaks to me
About the Fall Formal.
We keep the conversation
To jokes about math class
And cheers for Anne and Katia,
Whose graceless tap rendition
Of *42nd Street*
Draws ridiculous applause
From the crowd
And Barry's appreciative glance
At Katia's lumpy thighs.

"They did a great job, didn't they?"
He slides back in his seat.

"I don't know much about tap."

"Cool costumes, huh?"

"They made them themselves."

I look at Katia and Anne, arm in arm,
Panting, sweaty, grinning on the stage,

And think of the precise curtsy I will give on tour
After dancing the Little Swans
With Madison and Simone,
Wrapped in frothy castoffs from the real ballerinas.

After the show, they invite me

To go out with a group
Of Upton kids
For sweets at a trendy spot
Where ice cream costs almost as much
As my entire dinner
With Remington
Last night.

Barry takes us in his dad's Suburban.
Katia rides shotgun.
The rest of us cram in back,
Then into a giant corner booth
Where the boys order banana splits
And the girls junior sundaes, even me,
Anxiously counting rumpled dollars from my pocket.

Anne's face is still flushed from dancing,
Her eyes dramatic with mascara
That would never be allowed at Upton
In daylight.

The talent show judges
Awarded ribbons for most original act, funniest,
Best singer, best group,
Best costumes (won by Katia and Anne),

And a dozen other prizes.
Reminded me of those early grade-school soccer games
Where they didn't keep score
So there were no winners, no losers,
Just celebrations, laughter, messes of ice cream.

Nothing like the Jersey Ballet
With its endless auditions, eternal scrutiny,
The cruel knowledge that we can't all be
Enough.

College Fair Day at Upton

Is not like anything I have ever seen before.
My high school in Vermont had one harried adviser
Trying to get farm kids to consider UVM
Or one of the state schools somewhere else in New England
Or even just the idea of not milking cows
For the rest of their lives.

At Upton, the advisory staff,
A well-rehearsed corps de ballet,
Flaunts and flatters their prima students
Across a stage of college admissions tables
To lunches with corporate moms and dads
Eager to share their stories, mentor their youth
Into boardrooms and corner offices.

Everyone in their best blazers
For once not scoffing at the dress code,
Peacocks in burgundy and beige.

I walk along, self-conscious, confused,
Quoting my scores, accepting sheets of paper,
Feeling as uncertain a scholar
As I was a ballerina that first morning
In the Jersey Ballet studio,

While my classmates offer well-rehearsed answers,
Posture, pose
As if they all knew this was an audition
But no one had told
Me.

"Swarthmore has astronomy for you
And languages for me."
Katia pulls Barry's arm.

"I can't decide between Harvard and Yale."
Anne's mom went to one and her dad to the other,
Which makes her, apparently,
A bit like Madison and her ballet board dad.

I pull at the frayed sleeve of my blazer,
Wishing I had not returned Ruby Rappaport's
Designer castoff, a thousand times nicer
Than mine the day I bought it at Kohl's.

The college fair concludes

With advisory round tables.
Katia, Anne, and I listen
As one student after another
Describes something she learned,
He liked.

When my turn comes, I babble,
"I thought Swarthmore looked cool.
It has a dance program."
I catch a trace of chagrin
Beneath Katia's placid eyes,
Not unlike Tina and Kari
When I told them I was going away.

As if I was taking Swarthmore from her
When I expressly told my adviser
I wasn't interested in making these kinds of choices
Anyway.

A little angry at Anne
For the relieved expression
When I don't lay claim to anything Ivy League.

Surprised at the shard of myself
That's curious
What Swarthmore might really be like.

"I got the tattoo!"

Bess squeals into the phone.

"Where?"

"Thigh. Chickened out on going higher.
Dad might have killed me!"

I giggle aloud
So the others on the bus look up.
College Fair Day made me too late
For a safe ride with Ruby.

I don't tell Bess
About the Upton College Fair.
It seems unfair she couldn't have come,
Seen all the colleges with music programs, jazz bands.

"When are you inking that ballet slipper?"
Bess asks.

"I don't know where there's a tattoo parlor around here,"
I say.

I can't explain how Jersey and Remington,
Dancing on cruel cinder-block floors on tour,

Too many pairs of worn-out pointe shoes,
Sweat and sleepless nights of confusion
Have left a mark far more indelible
Than any needle could.

They are sending

Lisette, Bonnie, and Madison
To New York City
To audition for summer programs
At the most elite ballet schools.

Yevgeny smiles at me gently.
"You'll grow a lot studying here this summer,
Staying with the Medranos a while longer."

When I tell Mom and Dad,
I just say that they've asked me to stay
For the summer.

It's not a lie.

Everyone is thinking of being

Somewhere else.
The Upton crowd dreams of college,
The Jersey Ballet girls dream of bigger cities.
I've traveled all this way
To feel like I am staying
In place.

A freeze-frame photograph
A poster on a Vermont basement wall
A held pose.

I think this as I plié, jeté,
Rond de jambe en l'air,
Grand battement.
Left hand on the barre, then right.

With spring
Has come understanding.
I can read Yevgeny's subtle hand gestures,
Follow Shannon's barre combinations with relative ease,
Interpret Señor Medrano's heavy, accented commands.

We move to center for a new adagio.
Señor demonstrates with half steps in his worn, black shoes.

I try to focus on his directions
Instead of dissecting some uncertain dream,
Some desire
That has yielded me nothing
But second-best heartaches,
Ensemble roles.

I think how Remington would be
Engaged in the dance,
Not planning a moment, a breath
Beyond.

Press open my eyes, my ears.
Try to be here,
To be now.

April showers pound the road

As Señor Medrano drives home.

I am almost too tired to be afraid
Of his over-quick tugs of the wheel,
The other car headlights' distorted glares
Through sheets of rain.

From the corner of my eye, I see
Señor's grin.
Today in Variations class
I danced Aurora
Without a stop,
A misstep.

Danced to feel her body move
Without wondering what would come next,
Without wondering where I wanted to be
Or whether my wishes were right or wrong
Or ever coming true.

Fourteen delicate forward steps on pointe,
Fourteen genteel yet ever-growing circles of the hands

Without caring about the next day, the next hour,
The next audition.

The rehearsal schedule turns grueling

Again. In June, we will present
Variations,
Parts of the tour,
And some new dances
In a student concert
For family, friends.

Before that,
The company will perform
Coppélia.
Like *The Nutcracker*,
Another ballet based upon
A macabre Hoffman tale
About a doll come to life.

This time, though,
I will join the corps with Lisette, Bonnie, and Madison,
Not be buried amongst the snowflakes of C level dancers.

We four are invited to join the company class
On Saturdays,
Which no longer leaves time for afternoon interludes
With Remington.

He smiles at me
From across the studio.
My knees soften as usual.
I feel a pull in my heart
But can't quite see the direction.

At the too-short break
He comes to me.

"Denardio's tonight?"

"Okay." I nod.

When Remington meets me
At the dressing-room door,
My hair is still up,
My dress, rumpled, not replaced by chic jeans, tight top,
My nose shiny.

I don't understand what
Draws me to his dark eyes.
A marionette
Pulled, like Coppélia, on strings of another's making.

But today, I danced
Not in the back row
Not at the end of the line
Not just with girls
So much younger than I.

Those things I did myself

And I am smiling
As I ride on Remington's motorcycle.
Arms clenched around his muscled waist,
I squint against the wind pressing into my eyes
As mud spatters up from the road onto my pale pink tights.

The spring air is damp.
The still-bare trees, like awkward young dancers,
Hint at the promise of green,
Of future beauty.

Mom texts while I'm in bed with Remington.

The urgent buzz
Rouses me from my drowsy stupor.

"Can't you get it later?"
Rem kicks the covers.

"Just take a second."

The message wonders what dates I can spare
For some college visits
This summer.

"Your mom again?"
His eyes are knowing.

"She wants me to look at colleges."

"I want you, too."

I hold the silver phone in my hand,
Feel its weight,
Sleekness.
It says the time is nine p.m.
"You need to take me back to the Medranos'."

"Okay, okay."

Remington stands up
Slides into his jeans
Grabs me before I can reach my dress
Twirls me in his arms.

"Do an arabesque.
No, the other leg.
Not too high, just forty-five degrees,
Then pull your knee forward.
Can you drop your head down to touch it?"

In only my tank top and underpants
I point my toe,
Reach my leg back,
Move to his words.

As always,
Remington's ideas for dancing
Burn into my heart.

I am tired of making dances in this room

Only to see them performed by Lisette.
Only to watch him tell others about his successes before me.

But I cannot stop moving.

I stand outside the door

Of Professor O'Malley's office.

In my hand two short pages:
The story of a skeleton ballerina in a waiting room
Reading a book about a mythical, bosomy woman
And the man who cannot resist her
And the dance she dances
To try to be that girl.

My right hand will not knock on the wooden panel,
Will not try the brass knob.
My left hand clenches,
Wrinkling the sheets where dreams of ink
Are nearly as terrifying
As Yevgeny's eyes
When I arrive late to dance class.

Professor O'Malley is short.
A flap of gut bulges beneath his sweater.
His hands are small, ink-stained, lined.
But he lets me write my own dances.

Easter is a feast

At the Medranos'.
Señora cooks wildly,
Gestures at Julio and me
With flour-white fingers,
Speaking rapid-fire Spanish
Peppered with the occasional English phrase.

We sit at the kitchen table
Rolling hard-looking cookies in powdered sugar.

Julio smirks,
Flicks sugar at my face.
"You gonna eat any of these pebbles?"

"Don't!" I flick some sugar back,
Try not to meet Señora's eyes,
Which is easy, given her cooking frenzy.

"Papa will make the flan,
So that will taste okay."
He is wry, philosophical.

"Shouldn't you be practicing guitar
Before it gets too late?"

I give Señora my good-girl smile,
Stick my tongue out at Julio.

His eyes turn from silly to serious.
I think he knows what happens before
I come back home from Remington's
And I do not like to think
Of Julio
Imagining those things.

I shut my eyes.
Erase my smile.
Remind myself that Julio and I
Are both prisoners.
His chains are made of guitar strings
Held fast by his parents' desires
While I sometimes rail against bars of pink satin and mirrors,
Though I've half forgotten
Who wants this life I lead
Or who even really chose it to begin with.

I remember my shock

When I learned there was no Easter Bunny,
No Santa Claus.
Confronting my father in the front hall
Before we left for ballet class.

My informant was a first-grade friend, Jessica,
Whose parents were free-spirited, practical folks.
One April morning, Jess, quite matter-of-factly,
Pronounced the Easter Bunny a myth
"And the rest of that stuff, too."

Dad looked woebegone at my certainty
As if he had not expected me
To ever be wise,
To connect
The bags of bright-colored candy in the supermarket
With the same stuff in my big pink basket
Filled with grass as fake
As all it stood for.

Still, I almost cry
At the sight of my old Easter basket.

Señor and Señora

Clap with delight at my surprise.
Mom and Dad shipped the basket
Filled with treats and presents
Down to Jersey,
Where the Medranos kept it hidden
Until Easter morning.

Not until now
Do I regret
Missing Dad's egg hunt in the orchard,
Nannie's suntanned arms
Enveloping me in wafts of Shalimar and Avon skin cream,
Mom's worried musings
On if it was time to pour the glaze over the ham
Or whether the meat was still cold in the middle.

"What's this?"
Julio picks up a small white box
Labeled NORTHERN LIGHTS SWEETS.

"Dark chocolate caramels.
Want one?"
I hold them out,
Though I don't want to share.

There is a pair of gold earrings
Shaped like ballet slippers,
A book of poetry,
Jelly beans, licorice vines,
And those candy dots that come on rolls of white paper.

Presents fit for a girl of sixteen—or six.

Jessica's words waft over me.
"A myth . . . a myth . . . a myth . . ."

I am six years old again,
Standing dumbstruck before her
By the playground swings.

I am in the front row

This Saturday.
I pretend it is not because Lisette and Bonnie
Are auditioning in New York.

Try to put my heels gingerly on the floor,
Warm up slowly,
Feel my hips popping in and out
Of where they are supposed to be.

Yevgeny pauses beside me,
Concerned.

"Maybe you should get some physical therapy,"
He suggests.

From Jane?

I am good at being quiet
So I do not laugh
Out loud.

Remington invites me

Into the little studio.

"Can you help us out, Sara?"
His voice is casual.
Yevgeny stands by the stereo in the corner,
Cueing up music.
"You know a little about this dance."

I drop my bag by the door,
Barely able to nod,
Feel like I am passing through
A mythical gateway,
Entering a chapel.

"I want to work on a bit of pas de deux."

He leads me through steps
I pretend I have not committed
To heart. Takes my hands,
Passing them over and under his own
In the complicated pattern
We composed beside his bed.

Yevgeny watches, nods,
Makes the occasional suggestion
About helping me balance,
Smoothing Rem's steps.

In an hour, it is done.
I wipe the sweat from my forehead,
Which can barely contain its visions
Of our passing hands illuminated by stage lights.
Run to take a sip from the water fountain in the hall.

"Lisette said she can come for a late rehearsal
Tomorrow
When she gets back from New York,"
I hear Rem say to Yevgeny
As I come back through the door

To realize I am just Coppélia, a doll,
A substitute for Lisette's great talent.

As if what Remington does with me
Could ever be real, in his real world,
The way it is for me.

It turns out the stories of Greek mythology,
The most ancient epics that came before
Nory Ryan's Song
The Jungle
Great Expectations

The tales of muses, sirens,
Easter rabbits, Santa Claus,
Are all true.
And, most of all,
I am

A myth, a myth, a myth.

At Upton I find myself

Rifling through shelves
Of college guides, catalogs.

It seems like there are thousands.
My adviser said to look
For universities with dance programs.

I pull the Swarthmore brochure
From the section labeled ARTS.
Turn the pages, as if they could explain
How a school can grow dancers
On a green, leafy campus,
Inside grandiose buildings
Adorned with NO SMOKING signs.

There's a girl with a straight back,
Taut ponytail, bulging bag
That could easily hold ballet shoes.
She smiles out from page five.
And I grab a copy of the application,
Not just because it saves me from going
To morning math tutorial.

My cell phone pulses

As Ruby Rappaport races me
Down Harris Avenue,

Turning her head away
From the road
To point out a rainbow,
Mottled pink and yellow arches
Costuming the white-and-neon Rite Aid building
With a kind of grace.

A text from Bess.
Six words:

"On Easter I kissed Billy Allegra."

I picture them at the annual orchard Easter Egg Hunt,
Bending to grab the same bright, plastic egg
From the crook of a gnarled apple tree,
Brought together by the traditions
Of Darby Station, where, eventually,
Every path crosses another

If you don't go away.

I imagine their foreheads
Nearly touching,
Their sneakers damp from running through dewy fields.

I doubt Billy has discovered
The musical note,
Purple on Bess's thigh
Near the elastic of her underpants.

Should she feel any more sorry
Than Rem for continuing his curious friendship with Jane
Despite me?

I can't bring myself to feel anger,
Though the thought of their kiss
Dissolves the dream of returning home to Vermont,
To be the girl I was before,
Into another siren's island, another place
Where I have failed in courage, in voice.
Another myth of safe harbor.

"Sara, we're here."
Ruby taps my shoulder.

I look up to see the cracked asphalt,

The heavy, metal double door.

Realize I've been staring
At those six words
A long time
Without answering.

Lisette brings

A dog-eared paperback to the studio:
Nory Ryan's Song.
"It's a great story," she says.

A million notions scuttle through my mind,
Hopes for friendship, understanding.
I want to ask her how she feels
Doing the movements Rem teaches.
Instead . . .

"I don't want to dance anymore."
I hear my confession

To Lisette's
Upturned nose,
Dirty-blonde bun.
Her eyes round,
Like Coppélia's,
Astonished buttons.

I want to paint
Red circles on her cheeks—

Complete the costume
Of incomprehension.

But it's me
Who is Remington's toy
He can play with
Or abandon
On his whim.

I leave Lisette
With her well-read book,
Run into the dressing room,
Lock myself in a toilet stall,
Cry
As if every bone in my body
Were shattered.

When Señor Medrano finds me in the hall

I have managed to cover the dark circles
Beneath my eyes,
Dust my red, snuffling nose
With enough powder
To avoid curious looks.

"Bonnie, she is sick.
You will dance Aurora
On the tour this week."

A thunderclap. I grab
At a chance
Of silver linings.
A moment on center stage
Almost erases the memory
Of my confession to Lisette.

A thrill roils my stomach,
Rattles up my throat
To a catch in my breath.

"Uh-huh." I nod,

Then blush
At the speed of my reply,
My failure to ask what's the matter
With Bonnie or when she's coming back,
At how quickly I plan
To put off completing the Swarthmore application.

The girl who doesn't want to dance
Staring at a chance to be
Prima.

Every day is a flurry of extra practice—

Repeat, repeat, repeat.

Simone says Bonnie's not so much sick
As struggling with her hatred of her weight,
Now dangerously low.

I imagine her amidst the cats and chaos
Of her crowded house,
Or here between the perfection of Lisette
And the flamboyance of Simone,
Twisting the white elastic she keeps around her waist
Tighter and tighter until
Her body disappears like my voice
When I look too closely in the mirror
Without the pages of a notebook, a pen
To save me.

The *Sleeping Beauty* music
Burns into my brain as I développé, tendu, turn.
In their eyes I see them compare me
To Bonnie's absent form.

I fear the shadow of their disappointment
And, some nights, can no more connect
My reflection to the knowledge that I will be Aurora onstage

Than my heart to the desire I once had
To celebrate sixteen in pointe shoes.

In the dressing room on Tuesday night,
I scribble my fears
Onto the back of an old social studies assignment.

"What are you writing?"
Lisette peers over my shoulder.

Is there a graceful way
To cover my words with my hand?
Protect my secrets without losing
Her offer of friendship?

My toe slides along the front of my calf.
I release it at the very last moment,
Let it fly out, into the unforgiving open air
Of the stage.
My muscles its only hope
Against plunging to the ground.
Remember the slow, lenient moments
When the toe could touch the leg,
When there was safety in a preparation, a beginning,
The chance to fail had not yet become

A failure.

Sometimes, of course,

The movement is perfect,

The risk its own reward.

The step becomes

A dance.

Other times, it is the mottled stumbling

Of a human stuck to earth,

Of a dreamer half awake,

Too uncertain

To make a wish come true.

I turn over these words,

The page.

"Just some stupid stuff

For school," I say to Lisette.

At Señor Medrano's

I will type my notion

Into the computer keyboard.

Print a hard copy

On fresh, white paper.

“Denardio’s tonight?”

I ask Remington.
My voice, a little louder than I planned,
Turns a few heads
But I don’t see Jane.

Rem raps his cigarette pack
Against his palm.
Answer sliding slowly from his silky lips.
“Okay.”

I have never asked for anything before.
Never shown my want beyond the press of a thigh,
The strength of a glance.

But, later, sitting across from his distracted eyes,
Soaking in the oily smell of cheese,
Pizza crust singed in a busy brick oven,
My will dissolves.
I ask nothing,
Only whisper, when he stands,
Lifts up the helmets,
“I can’t tonight. I have too much homework.”

“Then why did you . . . ?”

I can't explain.

Is there somewhere, in the allegro beats of days ahead,
A time
When Remington will stop
Letting me huddle in his bed?

What will I become
If I stop waiting when he tells me to,
Show him the dances I write,
Ask for something different, something more
Than stolen kisses, secret afternoons,
Rem's voracious gazes
That do not fill me up?

"This is different."

Professor O'Malley rubs his chin
As he reads the page
I bring to him on Wednesday morning.

I cannot tell if he means worse
Or better.

But I double-check
That I've left the extra button on my blouse
Undone.
My blazer sits folded atop my backpack
By the door.

"What did you think of . . ."
I sidle up,
Bend my head beside his head,
Point to an unseen line.

He reads a passage aloud,
Thoughtful.
His breath smells like wintergreen.
His narrow mustache
A little greasy.
I wonder what it would feel like to
Have it brush against my lip.

"Sara?"

"What?"
I bleat
Like a stupid chorus girl,
Cowering as if he could read in my eyes
The temptation
To shift my weight
Against his shoulder.

On the corner of his desk
A photograph of three little girls
In summer bonnets,
Not unlike the hallway frame
Where my great-grandmother
And her sisters
Stare from beneath their heavy cloches,
On guard against lice.
I think his daughters in their finery
Guard Professor O'Malley
Against girls like me.

I am ashamed
Of the reason

I brought this page
To his office,
Of the button
Undone at my breastbone
And the time I spent brushing out my hair.

As if I were dancing, I feel my body separate
From my soul,
Watching from overhead
A girl who stands too close
To a man.

"I've, um, got to go."

My paper is still in his hand.
I do not take it back.
Just grab my bag,
Run, graceless, head bowed,
Down the long hall,
Out the dark oak door.

Past the safe green hedgerows
To the gritty street.

I do not even know what time it is
Or if I should have stayed longer at school
But when the bus comes,
I get on.
No matter two tattoo-smeared men who sit
In the front seat
Catcall and whistle
As I squeeze past their knees.

My face is numb, then ice, then fire

As the bus lumbers down
Harris Avenue.

Why did Remington kiss me
That first night at Denardio's?
Why couldn't he have said
My name
Out loud,
Made the moment
Syncopate,
Hesitate?

But then,
I didn't have to

Kiss him back.

Plié, tendu, rond de jambe, jeté

In my stylish gray leotard
With its thin straps, well-cut legs,
Fresh pink tights
Unencumbered by leg warmers.
Outside I look like the others now.

Once you learn the technique
Of joining a man in bed
It seems that it might stretch further
Than développés, splits, grand jetés.
And maybe you'll consider
Using that technique
On more than one boy

Until, like ballet,
The steps become
An act in themselves,
Separate from you,
And you forget who you are
All over again.

I have not called Bess

Since she texted about Billy Allegra.

She knows I've always liked him. Still,
I've been away so long.
I imagine she thought,
What was the harm?
It isn't as if I ever asked her
In all my emails and texts
About him.

I guess Kari, Tina, Bess, and I
All agreed
Billy's muscled arms, brown curls
Were something worth the gaze
Of any girl.
And so I dial.

"Why do you like swing music?"
I ask when she answers the phone.

"Why not?"

Her reply is bright, white,
Simple as an apple blossom,

Artful as a girl can be
Who has never braved a city bus,
Who reads only one book
All year long at school.

"It's up-tempo, romantic.
In those black-and-white movies with huge scores
Where every musician gets a chance to stand up,
Solo . . . A dream."

I know her dreams also stray
To the feel of a boy's hands
Exploring her breasts.
I know she would listen
If I told her
Everything I have learned
Since coming to Jersey.
But I cannot speak,
Cannot write
About that.

At the next stop on the tour

The floor of the school is hard as all the others
But I do not feel it
As I slide into Aurora's lacy tutu,
Watchful for Rem's eyes
At the dressing-room door.

Try to forget about boys,
About men,
Become the innocent sleeping beauty
Aurora was at sixteen.

The CD, well-worn from Bonnie's many performances,
Includes a few certain, predictable hesitations.
I build them into my dance,
Feel my arms swirl, my toes point,
Grabbing at celebration,
At dancing
For joy.

The little girl
In Ms. Alice's basement,
Whose friends celebrated,
Whose parents softly prodded,
Who wanted to be good,

Who became good enough to audition
For the chance to leave them all behind.

Before I know it
The music has stopped.
My dance has ended.

From the wings, Madison and I watch

Remington's dance,
Which Yevgeny has added to the tour program.

Lisette and Fernando,

Her head, bent forward.
Her arms, reaching back.
He draws her up into an arabesque.
She pulls her knee forward, head down again.
He grabs her hips, lifts her to the side.

Madison follows every move,
Her feet pointed as if
She would step onto the stage
Any instant.

When it is over, the applause
Crashes toward us
As if the kids in the audience
See, understand
This dance is special,
Different, made
On one of them

For them,
For us.

Behind me,
Already in his Papa Bear shirt,
Rem grabs my hand,
Gives it a quick squeeze.
He's called the dance "Country Duet."

I feel the electric joy
In his fingertips,
The rushed exhale
Of his elation.

Look up to where his moist eyes reach
From the wings
To Lisette's perfect curtsy.

Scurry away
To change into Mama Bear
For another kind of country dance.

The applause lingers

Like dust in bright sunlight
As Remington and I begin
Our bear promenade.

I let him lead me
Through the simple combination,
Watch, as usual,
Fernando support
Goldilocks Lisette's precise pirouettes.

Resist the urge
To step to center stage
Alone, claim my part
In Rem's dance.

The audience is still with us,
Laughing, cheering at the bears' silly antics,
Goldilocks's delightful arabesques,
Exploding when Lisette takes her bow.

In the back of the bus on the way home,

Remington sits beside me.
A grin hovers on his lips.
He laces his fingers playfully through mine,
Tilts his head.

I blush remembering my half-taken step
Toward Professor O'Malley,
Feeling the uncertain power
Of my words on the page.
I force the guilty image from my mind and, instead, accept
Remington's familiar invitation,

Endure his kisses, always too slippery,
Too wet.
His huge, wrapping embrace
Presses my shoulders.

Is he as changed
As I
By the storming applause
For the "Country Duet"?

The bus swerves around a sharp corner.
Brakes screech.

I slide across the green leather seat
Away from him.

Before he pulls me back,
I wipe the wetness from my lips,
Straighten my top.

"Remington?"

"Huh?" He's lighthearted,
Curling my legs across his lap.

The road straightens.
I see clearly as if they were typed
Onto the page of a book,
Two lines,
A question:

"Do you want a ballerina
Or a woman?"

I feel his body stop
His hand drops onto my leg.
He gives a little laugh,

The kind he used against Paul's questioning glares
At our first embrace months ago,
Across the table at Denardio's.

"What do you mean, Sara?"

My name coming from his lips
Makes me shudder
But I will not let him
See me cry.
"That's your answer?"

Rem rubs his hand against
The five-o'clock stubble forming
Along his jaw.
Looks past my shoulder out the window.

"Did you hear that applause today?"

My head is as cloudy as the night I never went to the movies
With Madison and Bonnie, but instead
Raced up the stairs to Remington's place.

I feel reckless, drunk, insane.
I want to grab his face,

Point his eyes at me,
Make him look.

"Why did you give my dance to Lisette?"

Now he turns away from the window,
Back to me, his endless lashes doing nothing
To soften the hardness in his brown eyes.

"It's not your dance."

In the months that she's been driving me

Along the avenues of Jersey,
Ruby Rappaport has had a dozen fights
With Adnan but

I don't think they have been anything like what happened
Between Rem and me
On the bus last night.

He is late to dance class on Monday,

Slipping in when the rest of us are already
Circling our legs in ronds de jambe.

I watch Remington's slow pliés
From the corner of my eye
Until Yevgeny's sharp critique of my timing
Jolts me back to my own dance.

After barre, we move to center, where
Yevgeny sets a brisk series of jumps across the floor.
Tombé, pas de bourrée, glissade, assemblé.
Chassé, chassé, chassé, tour jeté.

The dancers prepare, stepping through the combination
In bits and pieces, in silence.
I stand still, listen to the soft shushes and dull thuds
Of dancing before the music.
It's rhythmless and disjointed,
Full of false starts, abrupt stops,
Like Remington, alone in the small studio,
Or dancing round the corners of his dark apartment
With me.

I know I did not, could not have woven
The complex tapestry of hands over hands, and lifts to turns,

Or matched the steps and counts
That made the duet
Lisette and Fernando performed,
Yet

I know I am some part of that fabric—
There was some reason Rem wanted
To tangle his fingers with mine
And draw my legs across his lap
In the back of the bus last night.

After Variations class,
Fernando passes a group of us in the hall,
Suggests Denardio's.

Rem glances my way for one quick beat, turns to Fernando,
Nods.
Paul and Don and Galina
Agree.

I say I have too much homework
To spare the time.

Julio is putting his guitar away

When Señor and I get home.

"Cards?" he asks.

The question feels so normal, so mundane,
I can only shake my head, refuse,
In silence so the tears won't escape
Before I reach the safety, solitude, home
Of musty carpet, slippery quilt.

I leave my blazer in my room on Tuesday,

Parade through the halls of Upton
Bereft of burgundy adornment,
Hoping someone will catch me, stop me,
Tell me what to do.
But the headmaster is not in his office when I walk by.

In math tutorial, I try
But the numbers blur
Too much in my heart to add
Together.

I put away my pencil.
Take out a pen.
Write on a fresh piece of paper:

"I will never go back
To Remington's bed."

In clear, blue ink.
Words
To make it
Real.

Rem and Jane are talking in the doorway

Of her office
Before class in the afternoon.
They seem to freeze as I pass.

I can't resist turning back to them
Before I go into the dressing room.

A few minutes later, Jane comes through the door.
"He wants to talk to you."

Her eyes look half victorious yet half sorry
So I can't sort out what Remington could have told her
About our country duet—whether he had any interest
In discussing it with me or if Jane,
With her health-care-professional practicality,
Just told him that he should.

"He wants a lot of things," I say.

Jane laughs
The kind of laugh
You're supposed to join in with

If your heart isn't an open blister,
Raw and bleeding inside a new pointe shoe.

In Variations class, Yevgeny partners me

With Remington.
I lose my balance
At the first touch of his hand,
Our duet an impossible attempt
At an impossible conversation.

It's a slow, languorous dance
From Balanchine's *Four Temperaments*,
With its strange, discordant music
That captures some part of what used to be
Between Remington and me
But maybe never truly was
Or slowly faded, a drawing curtain, a song
Dwindling to silence—

Sanguine, phlegmatic, choleric, melancholy.

Like the moods, the fateful journey
Of Milton's Adam and Eve
Traveling from paradise
To another kind of dance for two.

After, I write down for Professor O'Malley

A long piece
About chords and harmonies,
Dancers and dances.

How making a dance is very different
From learning it,
Dancing it,
Performing it with someone
Or before footlights.

Like a word
Read aloud
Sounds different in every voice.

Professor O'Malley scrawls
"Keep writing"
In his spider handwriting, red pen.
Though he does not ask me
To stop by his office.
And I think, maybe,
He is right.

I've spent a year pretending,

So why should it be any different
Writing a new myth—
One where Remington and I
Never were?

That I am still the innocent girl who sat on fence posts,
Followed a dream others dreamed for her,
Danced on summer sand without
Dipping her toes
In the water?

I try to console Julio,

Who is fighting with Simone
Over some misunderstood text,
Innocent omission.

Though I do not tell him
How much it hurts to see Remington
Rehearsing with Lisette in the small studio,

Or how I miss his hands,
The safety of his enveloping presence,
Sheltering his muse—

A role that seems to weaken in my memory
In a way the steps of Aurora's dance
Will never fade.

"Rummy 500?" I shove my sorrow
Into a punch at Julio's shoulder.

"I've got to weed the front walk
Before Mama gets home."

I leave the cards on the sticky yellow tablecloth
As Julio laces up his boots,

Goes out through the garage.
I should go out and help him
But instead
I walk past the abstract paintings,
Up the steps to my bedroom.

Sort through my half-dry leotards,
Separate the new gray ones from the other colors.
Pull one across my chest as I stand before the mirror,
Wonder if I could have told Remington
Whether I am a ballerina or a woman
Myself.

May becomes all preparation

For the final performance.
Notices cling to the bulletin board:
The order of dances,
Rehearsal calls,
A local newspaper clipping featuring Lisette,
Smiling, hair brushed out and long,
Announcing her acceptance as a junior apprentice
To a New York ballet company.

Bonnie is back,
So I will not dance Aurora
In June,
Though I am glad to see the hint of rosy roundness
In her still over-lean face.
Lisette and Fernando will officially premiere
Remington's prize-winning dance.
Madison, Simone, and I will bob and sway as Little Swans.
I'll dance the bears' duet
With Remington.

When you dance with a partner

You have to learn
When you should be the one to begin a step,
When your partner times the landing of a lift.

I've been studying hard
For final exams at Upton,
With more energy than I had
When my nighttime hours were lost in Rem's bed.
I sit on the floor in the hall of the ballet school,
Legs in a side split,
Book propped against my dance bag,
Not wasting the time while I wait for a ride
With Señor Medrano.

Still, sometimes I look up from the page,
Distracted by the music snaking
Around the corridor
From the small studio.
Some nights the CD player sashays through the Bach cantata
That makes me think of the orange chairs
In his living room, the dusty smell
Of a brown afghan, the gorgeous feel
Of skin on skin.

I wonder what steps he is molding
Onto ballerinas,

If he'll ever make a dance that could explain
Who led, who followed
When it was Remington
And me.

Ruby and Adnan

Are arguing about summer plans again.
She zooms down Harris Avenue
At a speed that matches her frustration.

"Stop!" I shout
As the traffic signal turns red
And the taillights of the car before us
Flash.

Ruby jams the brake,
Stopping the red convertible a second
Before what seemed like an inevitable
Crash.

"Oh my God, I'm sorry, Sara.
I didn't mean . . ."

I think of Rem's magnetic smile that night at Denardio's,
Of Bess and Billy on that Easter afternoon,
The momentum of a turn,
The rush of reality as you slam on the brake,
The force of gravity
That stops pirouettes and pulls arabesques down.

The light turns green again.
Ruby tenderly taps the gas,
Signals to move right, into the slow lane.

"It's okay."

Different test schedules mean
This is the last day Ruby can drive me to the studio.

Tomorrow, I'll ride the awful city bus,
Still terrified,

Though it occurs to me that
I have never asked
To get a driver's license,
Which would mean
Another test to take,
Another world to understand.
But then, sometimes
I could drive myself
Somewhere.

I imagine my bedroom

In Darby Station.

Think of painting it shadow gray
With a great rainbow across one wall,
Asking Dad to build bookcases,
Hang one bright brass hook
Up high on the ceiling
For a single pair of pointe shoes.

“Thinking of coming home,”

I text Bess.

She calls instantly, squealing.
“Senior year’s going to be great!”
She says lots more,
Starts planning a welcome-home party,
Checking dates for the fair
“So you can finally get that tattoo.”

I interject “mm-hmms”
At regular intervals,
An enthusiastic metronome.

And she, as consistent,
Prattles only of happy, easy things.

Bess, my childhood friend,
With whom I shared so many dreams,
Imagined so many tomorrows,
Who cannot envision anything
For my return except
The resumption of every old, familiar plan,
Forgiveness for everything
That happened while we were apart.

Do I need more forgiveness—
For feeling so different, so drawn, so distant—
Than she?

But I just say,
"This all sounds great! Thanks!"
Even though every book at Upton
From *Heartbreak House* to *Paradise Lost*
Tells a story of how you can't really go back
To anyplace.

Mom emails a long list

Of colleges to visit this summer.
I look it over as I fold my Upton uniforms,
Clothes she mostly chose, sent
To Jersey with me last fall.

Twist the unraveling shoulder seam
Of the cheap maroon blazer
She persuaded me to buy last August.

"I know you're busy at work,"
I write in reply.
"I've made a list, too.
Maybe I'll plan a trip
With Dad."

I try to imagine long afternoons
Without ballet classes, rehearsals,
Standing in damp sand,
Watching the little Allegra girls,
Now all one year taller,
Splash and giggle and pretend sometimes
To be ballerinas.

The Medranos are confused

When I try to explain
Into the chasm of half-understood English
That this is not their fault, that they have been very kind.

Julio interjects
The occasional Spanish phrase
In my support,
His thick brows furrowed,
Replacing a guitar string,
Not looking up at me.

"Okay, okay," Señor says at last.
"Julio, he will miss you.
We all miss you.
You a nice girl."
He gives my back a firm pat.

Señora stands up.
"I make coffee,
Those little cookies you like."

Now Julio chuckles.
I catch his eye.
"Rummy?"

He lays his guitar in its case.
"I'll get the cards."

"I'll miss you,"
I say as he shuffles, deals.
"It's been fun having a little brother."

"Little brother!" Julio drops the deck,
Punches my arm.
"I've got six inches on you!"

"Just deal!"
I punch him back,
Relieved to hear Señora announce
She doesn't have enough butter
To make the cookies.

School ends in early June at Upton

So I ride to the studio
With Señor Medrano
Every day.

Tendu and stretch.
Join the occasional company class
To fill the morning hours
Before the other students arrive.

Even though I won't be there for senior year,
Begin working my way
Through the Upton summer reading list.
Though, at night, *The Thorn Birds*
Still tempts.
It is hard to sleep alone
All the time.

One afternoon, I find the courage
To tell Yevgeny I'll be going home.
He pats my head.
"Perhaps we should have sent you
To the audition in New York this spring."

I don't know how to answer

Through my pride.
Perhaps I should have asked
To go to New York with Bonnie and Lisette
Instead of staying silent.

A kind of panic wafts over me,

Like the moment your partner lets go your hand
And you have to balance alone in arabesque
Or spin a pirouette
Without his palms against your waist;
The moment the penny leaves your fingertips
Bound for the wishing well
And you wobble, uncertain,
That you envisioned the right dream.

I want to turn time in reverse,
Retract my farewells,
Reclaim the dream everyone
Dreamed for me
For so long . . .

But only for a moment,
A heartbeat.

Now, I draw my chin up,
Make my voice loud.
"Thanks, Yevgeny."
I even say his name.

The sky is hazy

The Saturday of the final student performance,
The air unusually humid for June.

I've come to the theatre with Señor
So, as usual, I am early.

But Bonnie and Simone will be here soon.
Lisette, Madison, Fernando,
And Remington, who came to the dress rehearsal last night,
Wrapped in his favorite plaid shirt
To accept everyone's congratulations
On his commission to make a dance for the company
Next year.
Rem, wide hands clasped together,
Exuberant gaze tilted politely downward,
Not casting about for Jane
Or me.

Standing at the portable barre in the middle of the stage,
I work through half a dozen grand pliés.
My arm is softly rounded, fingers graceful
As I bend my knees, hold my turnout,
Allow my heels to come slowly

Off the floor. My heart aches a little
With my shins.

This performance may be on the grandest stage
I will ever grace, the last time I dance
Sewn into tulle and satin.

But I have stopped wanting
A life without words beyond
Fat romances to fill the moments
Between dances
That make me consider pressing my thigh
Against anyone in hopes
Of feeling my worth.

I've collected applications for half a dozen colleges
With dance programs, literary magazines.
Or I may choose someplace
Entirely different,
Someplace I haven't found yet, though
I am certain when I get there
I will know how to drive.

The thought makes my breath come sharp,

My eyes as bright
As the dancers around me
Swinging their legs, pinning up their hair,
Preparing for the radiance of the stage.

From the wings, I watch

Bonnie's beautiful Aurora,
Lisette and Fernando.

Then it's my turn:
The Little Swan in the middle
Framed by Simone and Madison.
Heads angled symmetrically
We piqué, plié, pas de chat,
End in tight fifth positions
On the music's final plinking note.

We step forward to curtsy
A révérence nearly the same
As we do at the end of a class,
Offering the audience our best
Vaseline-slick smiles, well-sprayed buns, sucked-in guts,
Gratitude for their applause.

We are the last variation before intermission.
We pose center stage as the footlights dim.
The houselights rise,
Revealing glimpses of the audience standing, stretching—
Friends, teachers, families, including Mom and Dad,
Who drove to Jersey early this morning,
Their Volvo trunk empty,

Ready to fill with the boxes I've packed.

Whispers of conversation slip
Between the folds of the closing curtain.

Simone and Madison release my hands,
Relax their shoulders, unglue their grins.
But I stand there a minute longer,
Back straight, neck long,
Left foot front, right foot crossed behind,
Smiling at the streaked beige satin of the curtain lining,
The echo of applause,
The tickle of lace against my legs,
The heat on my cheeks.

I know,
For Lisette, for Rem, this stage is a paradise found;
For Bonnie, an altar at which she sacrifices.

The curtain closed, the work lights come up.
Stagehands sweep.
Dancers rush to change into their next costumes.

In my head, I choreograph a poem
About reverence.